HARD
TO BE
KING

Oso Avon

NEWMAN SPRINGS PUBLISHING
320 Broad Street
Red Bank, NJ 07701

First originally published by Newman Springs Publishing 2021

ISBN 978-1-63881-335-4 (Paperback)
ISBN 978-1-63881-336-1 (Digital)

Printed in the United States of America

I'd like to dedicate this to my children and my God children, to 19th Street, and to Avon.

The sunlight peered through the window and danced on the coffee table as the sounds of summer invaded the dimly lit room. Quan scanned the room highlighted with accomplishments in the form of lavish amenities. Tears streamed profusely down his pure dark face as he gripped his gun and exhaled. *If only I can push these thoughts out of my mind*, thought Quan. The experience was unmentionable, and Quan was determined not to live through it, mentally or physically. Not only that, but not to hear it mentioned by no lips and no mouth ever. The more he thought, the tighter he gripped his gun and longed for it all to end. This certainly wasn't the way he imagined it all ending, but something had to give, and some demons are just too big to fight.

Across town, Trey drove erratically and carelessly through the kid-filled city streets that he usually loved so much. The police sirens wailed endlessly in the close distance, but Trey could only look ahead. He could only press forward, faster and faster. His silver BMW screeched and yelled throughout the voyage to his destination. Ab being the only other occupant of the vehicle was scared for his very life without the courage to say a word. Trey raced toward his life-long friend and partner in crime, and although he didn't know exactly why, he certainly knew something wasn't right. Trey persistently ignored the police's orders to halt as he turned the corner viciously, just shy of hitting a pedestrian. Poor guy wasn't so lucky at the expense of the police who hoped to capture Trey's freedom.

Quan had finally reached breaking point when he realized there were footsteps stampeding up the stairway toward his door. He hastened his decision, for he knew that it was Trey; and although he loved Trey like a brother, he couldn't turn back. He gently placed the

5

gun to his head without closing his eyes or even bracing himself for the unimaginable. Quan eased the trigger until the gun sent shock waves out into the hallway to Trey and Ab who rushed up the stairs. As they burst through the door, weapons drawn, the sight weakened Trey instantly. His boy lay lifeless on the expensive rug as his life escaped into the atmosphere. Before Trey could reach the pool of blood and matter that was once Quan, the police came storming in and it all became a blur.

Within a few short weeks, Trey and Quan's world had been turned upside down. What seemed like everything was being turned into nothing so rapidly. A few weeks back, Trey sat in his Manhattan condo just a few short miles away from the city that he thrived and prospered in—Newark, New Jersey. He faced a conflict he had no resolution for. The love of his life, Niki, wanted desperately for him to leave the drug trade and all that came with it while it was the only thing he knew and was good at. Aside from this, Quan, who was all that mattered to Trey beside Niki, would be lost without him.

Trey lived a secret life to appease his love. He was forced to invest in legitimate businesses so that he could explain his wealth and income to Niki legally. He knew she wanted a better life for him—for them—and he was truly torn. From barber shop franchises to soul food kitchens and real estate, Quan had Newark littered with his ideas and investments. Too bad it was all a lie.

A few short months ago, when things were more so normal, Quan and Trey sat on opposite sides of the same street, speaking to each other on their cell phones respectively. They both watched the flow of traffic and all the people who passed by. This elaborate sequence of events was all to enter the barber's shop. Easier said than done for two of the biggest suspected drug traffickers and murders within this zip code. Quan and Trey just wanted to rest assured that no one watched their moves. They both signaled one another and exited their vehicles.

As soon as they reached the safety of the shop, they went to the back room and closed the door. "Ay, man, this fucking Joe hit us hard with this," said Quan pounding a fist in his opposite hand. Trey just nodded in agreement. Joe was one of the old school hustlers that didn't have the sense to turn over the crown to the up and coming nation of successors. He went to war with all that stood in his way and won, mostly. Joe had cops, judges, politicians, and even city officials in his pocket so his influence seemed endless. Most of the others folded, lay dead, or joined his team with a respectable title to avoid being demolished. Trey and Quan were about to do neither.

The latest shipment in from Ricardo had been intercepted by Joe. To add insult to injury, Joe packaged the dope, labeled the bags "Customer Appreciation," and handed it out free all over the city. This move was both reflective of a great war strategy and business. After all, it would strengthen customer loyalty. Aside from this, the amount of the shipment would financially cripple Trey and Quan for at least a month. Or so Joe hoped at least. Although it hurt them financially, it didn't cripple them; but it did, however, leave them in a stage of drought. This also caused their customers to stray due to lack of supply.

Quan rambled on and on angrily, while Trey sat silently and thought. "So what up, nigga, what we gon do?" Quan's words brought Trey back to reality.

"Violence," was his simple reply. Trey got up out the chair and mumbled to his best friend while moving toward the door, "Do what you feel on this."

With that, the meeting was adjourned. Before Trey could make it to his car, Quan was on the phone calling Ab and Dee.

Trey nestled himself comfortably back into his vehicle as he flipped open his phone to call Niki. He wanted to escape the thoughts of his reality long enough to enjoy a lunch with her. Whatever Quan would do would be deadly and immediate. Knowing the way the streets talked, Trey wanted to be right by Niki's side when it went down to avoid suspicion. "What's up, babe?" Niki harmonized as she picked up the phone on the second ring. Her excitement to hear from Trey was evident in her voice.

"He hungry and he don't want to eat alone," Trey nonchalantly replied, speaking of himself in the third-person.

Niki, realizing her pleasant tone and demeanor wasn't returned, shot back, "Well, he needs to pick his lady up promptly."

Trey smiled silently. With no reply, he just closed the phone and pulled out in traffic toward his destination.

Niki dressed quickly, for she knew her man would be there shortly. She and Trey grew up together in an apartment building in their old neighborhood. He had the biggest crush on her coming up, but Niki's mom, Trina, always hated Trey and was extremely strict so they never ran in the same circle. Although Niki lived in the building, she lived a different life from private school to structured summer camps and activities, instead of the local haunts and hang outs. That always commanded Trey's attention and interest. Trey wasn't exactly a ladies' man, but he was popular. Quan, on the other hand, was both. His dark chocolate skin and hazel eyes were just the unique combination to acquire the young women. As he grew older, he honed in on his quality to have, dispose of, and manipulate women.

Within minutes, Trey's horn was blowing as Niki made her way out the door. As she exited her apartment and went to the hallway to catch the elevator, she could still hear Trey on the horn. This infuriated her, and he knew it. She would make sure and give him a piece of her mind when she got in the car. Niki was coming out the building, squinting her eyes and biting her bottom lip, while staring at Trey so he would stop blowing the horn. He felt her eyes piercing his skin but didn't stop until she opened the car door. As Niki got in, Trey smiled playfully and tried to kiss her. She wasn't impressed.

"Babe, pull around back so I can get my car, I'm driving today. Oh, and lunch is on me," Niki added as she closed the car door. Trey was glad to hear it, and immediately carried out the request. Not that driving or paying would be an issue, but his attention would be divided with what was going on with Joe and whether he made the right decision by leaving Quan to handle it.

Niki had just purchased a CL Mercedes that complimented her style and taste so much. She enjoyed driving it through the city so much, she learned to despise the passenger seat. She truly embodied success. She was in grad school for her master's in finances. Trey paid her generously as his financial advisor and accountant for all of his legitimate investments. Niki proved to be good for Trey on every level. In keeping up the front of acting as a law abiding citizen, she generated just as much revenue for him legally as he made illegally. It truly was a good combination. It was the love of the game that kept him entangled as a player. Not to mention it kept him connected to Quan through the friendship they shared since they were kids in the after school program.

Trey blocked out Niki's aggressive driving and offbeat singing as he pondered his next move like a well-machined chess player. This Joe thing was truly getting out of hand and could no longer be handled amicably. Ricardo, Trey's supplier, was afraid that his business would suffer a backlash and threatened to cut Trey off if he brought heat. Niki pulled up short at what she thought to be one of their favorite restaurants, Sahanalulu's. Trey secretly hated this place, but it was where they had their first date, and he knew how important it was to her. He forced a smile on his face as he unlocked the door to exit.

*****

Quan sat in the rear of the barber shop, anxiously awaiting Dee and Ab's arrival. He had the plan all gathered. Through a few phone calls, and a couple promises of some cash and dope, he secured information on one of Joe's main girls. Coincidently, Quan had sexed the woman's daughter a few times before she went to the navy. He recorded the event and the tape fell into the wrong hands, only to ruin the girl's reputation in the hood. Quan planned on running in the woman's place and forcing her to lure Joe there so they could trap him. Ab and Dee walked in to catch Quan's devilish grin take control of his handsome face.

"What up nigga? Who got to die?" Ab coldly asked as Dee finished up on a chicken bone.

Quan stood up and satisfactorily replied, "Joe bitch ass, now let's be out."

The three drove briskly to Cheryl's place as Quan briefed the two on the plan. Cheryl was an older beautiful woman that dressed like a movie star. She lived like a true mistress with all the glamour and local fame attached. All visitor's had to be buzzed into Cheryl's apartment building to gain entry. The three men sat impatiently outside, waiting for the perfect opportunity to surprise her.

Before the street talk and lies could fill the vehicle, that opportunity presented itself in the form of a Chinese delivery man. The small man waited in front after announcing himself through the voice box mounted on the front door. As his customer opened the door, Quan, Ab, and Dee pushed their way through, not looking at anyone in particular. Although the customer looked puzzled, the look on these men's faces were enough to deter him not to ask any questions and gather his food without interference. Before long, there was a knock at the door.

Cheryl, who was not expecting visitors and also hadn't buzzed anyone in, wrinkled her eyebrows and asked, "Who's there?" She moved deliberately to the door and repeated the question.

"It's me," Dee softly spoke through the door, clutching his gun tightly while gritting his teeth. Quan and Ab fought back laughter as Cheryl fumbled with the lock.

"Me who?" Cheryl attempted to put the chain on and crack the door to see who it might be. Bad idea. With one forceful push and a follow-through came three deadly men. Quan quickly snatched her up and swiftly slapped her across her face with his gun to express the seriousness of the situation. Dee closed the door and Ab quickly ran to the kitchen to grab a chair. Before he could return with the chair to execute his responsibility in the plan, he heard another slap.

Cheryl was completely caught off guard and could hardly catch her breath as she lay flat on her back with Quan towering over her. She recognized him immediately and began worrying about her daughter.

"Look, bitch, one time I'm a ask you and that's it. Say you don't know and I'm a start squeezing." Quan slowly spoke through his teeth with a sadistic mumble. Before she could register the information, Ab snatched her off the floor and placed her in the chair. "Where's that funky ass pimp of yours, Joe?" Quan stared at Cheryl to read her body language as she shook her head as if she were confused.

"I never know, he calls when he's on his way. I don't have a way to contact him." Cheryl began mustering courage to talk back to this kid that she always hated. "And even if I knew—"

She wasn't able to finish before another blow was delivered. The only recourse was for Cheryl to close her eyes and exhale as pain and agony overcame her. "All right, since you wanna play around, I just thought of two other things I could be doing." Quan moved in closer and placed the gun to her head. Cheryl opened her eyes to the gun's barrel and the boyish face, and she could only smile. Ab, knowing his friend, handed Quan a small pillow off the couch and turned away. Quan placed the pillow to the side of Cheryl's head and squeezed. Blood and matter immediately littered the couch and wall as her body collapsed and slumped. Dee turned from the bloody sight and vomited. This was a sign of weakness and would not be forgotten. Quan and Ab looked at him in disgust and began moving toward the door for their exit.

*****

Niki and Trey sat across from each other in the restaurant with serious faces and cold stares as they both attempted not to flinch. Trey slit his eyes tighter and began growling under his breath, and Niki burst out into laughter. Trey's face loosened up and he followed in a hearty laugh. They laughed uncontrollably for a couple of minutes before the waitress interrupted with a gentle hello. When she realized she had both of their attention, she began, "Sorry ma'am, but he won." She softly chuckled. "The good news is the gentleman in the corner section sends over a bottle of your favorite drinks and says your meal is on him," the waitress continued while pointing over to Joe.

Once he could see he had both of their attention, Joe held up his glass in a toasting motion and revealed all his beautiful teeth. Niki, who recognized Joe as one of her mother's friends, smiled and waved back pleasantly. Trey, on the other hand, coldly stared for a few seconds before moving any. Trey couldn't act or react the way he wanted because Niki wouldn't understand why he would qualify as

Joe's rival, especially if he was only an up and coming entrepreneur. As Trey slowly realized where he was, he stretched a grin across his face and smiled back. He quickly accessed the odds and decided they were tremendously in Joe's favor.

Joe had three tables pushed together with at least twelve men in his party. There was no win. At least nine of the men wore weapons like an everyday tie. "Excuse me, baby," Trey spoke to Niki as he held his smile and made his way over to Joe's area. As he neared the table of his enemy, Joe's men began reaching for their weapons. Joe motioned for them to stop.

"Be cool, boys. Baby boy is a smart man, he ain't no gangsta," Joe spoke sarcastically as he watched Trey. "I figured with the recent hit you boys took, you could use a little help paying for dinner." Joe chuckled as his men chimed in behind him. Trey was in a no-win situation. Here was his enemy, openly bragging that he was responsible for one of the biggest hits on his crew, yet Trey couldn't do anything. "Look here, Baby boy, you ain't got enough bread to buy a decent gun, so I know you ain't packing. So lemme tell you what you gon do." Joe spoke to Trey as he watched Niki and smiled. "Reach in them fucking broke down pockets of yours and pull that cell phone out. Lay it on the table in front of me and walk away."

Trey stood as his blood boiled within him.

"I don't ask twice, nigga." Joe raised his voice slightly while keeping his eyes locked on Niki. Realizing defeat, Trey reached in and placed his phone in Joe's drink and turned to walk away. "Ay," Joe called out as Trey attempted to walk away. "That's a pretty young lady you got there, son, take care of her." Again, Joe's men riddled the room with laughter as Trey made his way back to Niki.

Trey sat down at the table, feeling defeated and frustrated. Joe truly had the upper hand. He stripped Trey of his phone so he couldn't call or even text his location to have his boys show up. He could do no planning whatsoever to conquer the moment at hand. However, Joe may have acted against him while he was with Niki and helpless. The thought alone infuriated Trey. He was truly responsible for his lady's life and well-being, and his enemy had him at his mercy.

Niki spoke, smiled, chuckled, and ate without Trey's undivided attention. He tried as hard as possible to relax, but he just couldn't. Even when Joe got up to leave, Trey's mind worked in overdrive. *Was he going to be outside waiting for them? Would he follow Niki and Trey?* The suspense was too much for Trey to handle. Niki felt Trey rushing the lunch along, and although she tried to be passive, it was far too noticeable.

Joe seemed to rush out in a hurry with all his men. One minute they were laughing and chattering, and the next, Joe threw money on the table and rushed out with his entourage. Little did Trey know that Joe not only received the news about Cheryl, but suspected he somehow ordered the hit.

*****

Joe arrived at the scene in just enough time to see the coroner carrying Cheryl away. He held his head low. Somehow, he knew he was responsible. Cheryl was truly special to him and could get anything she wanted and needed. Trey would pay for this. Joe reached in his suit pocket and pulled out Trey's cell phone and stared at it blankly as the coroner pulled away from the curb and navigated away from the crowd. Silence controlled the vehicle as his men waited for their leader to speak the first words. No one dared speak out of turn, for they could see the anger and hurt in Joe's face. The ringing of Trey's phone broke the silence in the vehicle.

Joe snapped out of his daze and flipped the phone open without speaking. As he put the phone to his ear, chattering could be heard in the background. Quan immediately began speaking, "The heat is on! We hit 'em where it hurt, my nigga." Joe had heard enough. Somehow he assumed Trey ordered the hit to get back at him for the restaurant episode. Joe assumed Trey knew since he couldn't protect Cheryl, she would be an easy target. He opened up the car window and dropped the cell phone out and ordered his driver to pull away.

Quan stared at the phone as the line went dead. "What up, nigga?" asked Ab as they sat, proud of their accomplishment.

"I don't know. I called Trey to let him know the move went down and…well, something didn't seem right." Ab and Dee shrugged their shoulders simultaneously and probed immediately.

"Chill, just chill," Quan interrupted. "He probably with Niki and couldn't talk." This sounded like a reasonable explanation to each man as they dismissed their worries. "Now, back to your bitch ass." Quan redirected his attention to Dee. "How you gon throw the fuck up?"

Dee smirked and rolled his eyes bashfully as he was caught off guard. Ab stared out the corner of his eye. This was truly his friend, but he had lost respect for Dee at what occurred back there. There was always something about him that didn't seem right for their line of work.

*****

Trey pulled up in front of Niki's house with a screeching halt. He insisted on driving due to his uneasy feeling. Niki sat with her seat belt clenched tightly to the seat. By now, she could sense something was wrong but knew her man well enough to wait before asking. She noticed that he went the longest way possible to reach her house, but drove in a hurry, which made no sense to her. As Trey shifted the car in park and unfastened his seat belt, he kissed his lady and jumped out to run to his car. Niki shook her head silently and made a mental note to ask about this strange turn of events later. This was so unlike him.

Minutes later, Trey searched frantically for a pay phone. He needed to reach out to Quan to get guys over to Niki's, just in case Joe had followed them and was planning a move. Also, in the back of his mind, he questioned his judgment on letting Quan handle the situation without his consent. Quan came up with endless ideas on getting money, but Ab was the specialist on war in their crew. He was always known for beef in the hood and always seemed to emerge victoriously with both his life and freedom.

Trey realized how hard it was to find a pay phone now as he circled the block three and four times. He also worried about what secrets would be revealed through his phone that would make him vulnerable to Joe. Trey spotted someone he knew from around the way and pulled right over.

"Yo, my man." He rolled down the window and yelled out. As the tall slender man turned and recognized Trey, he began smiling harder and harder.

"What up, boss?" he affectionately replied as he made his way over.

"Rock, I need to use that jack right quick, man." Trey cut their greeting short. "Tell your chick you gon hit her right back."

Rock terminated his call without an explanation and handed the phone over to Trey, just as he had asked, "You peace, man?" Trey didn't waste time responding. He dialed Quan's number as quickly as possible.

"Yooo." Quan picked up on the first ring.

Trey exhaled and spoke quickly. "My nigga, where you at?"

Quan, recognizing Trey's voice responded, disappointed, "Man, I thought you was new pussy." He chuckled.

As serious as the situation was, Trey couldn't help but let out a laugh. He knew his friend all too well, and if money wasn't on his mind, it was certainly women. "Dog, I need you to get Ab and Dee over to Niki's and meet me at White Castle on Elizabeth Ave., like ASAP."

Quan didn't question it. He responded quickly, "Done."

Rock stood there puzzled the entire two minutes.

"My nigga, good looking, if there is anything I can ever do… holla." As quickly as Trey had appeared, he disappeared as Rock stood on the curb contemplating his offer.

*****

Trey sat impatiently in the White Castle's parking lot, looking out the windows for Quan. He parked almost two blocks away by habit. For some reason or another, there was always a reason for him to watch his step. If not the cops, it was his only enemy that qualified as a threat; or stick-up kids. As much respect as Trey and Quan had, history always revealed that stick-up would try anybody. He could see his boy in the distance, and his pace quickened. He hoped Ab and Dee were in position at Niki's, just in case.

Dee was questionable, but Trey knew Ab would die for Niki or any other cause that he and Quan deemed worthy. Quan came through the door and couldn't help but stop at some young ladies at a table, flirting before coming over.

"Yo, man, not now!" Trey yelled out drawing attention to himself and the situation.

Quan turned down his charm and made his way over. "Son, where your phone at?"

Trey waived his hands quickly and nodded toward the stool next to him. "This nigga, Joe," Trey didn't even know where to begin. Joe's name inserted the seriousness back into the conversation for Quan.

"Speaking of that nigga, come outside and let me spit at you."

Trey watched his friend closely and followed closely behind.

Minutes later, Trey cupped his head in his hands as he listened to what he missed. He inwardly admitted it was an excellent strategy but that the timing was terrible. Or was it? Trey wasn't sure he wanted to claim responsibility for what happened to Cheryl. Everyone knew how much she meant to Joe, and the term "hitting him where it hurts" was truly an understatement. Someone would definitely pay.

"Son, you did your thing, my nigga," Trey offered his hand as Quan accepted and they hugged in celebration. Truth be told, Trey felt uneasy about the whole situation. He even briefly thought of calling a truce with Joe but decided against it. This would only be construed as a sign of weakness, and Joe would capitalize on the moment. *Maybe Joe would think it was someone else,* Trey thought wishfully. *After all, I was in the restaurant with him when this happened, and he knew it.*

Trey tried hard to convince himself, but he knew Joe's history ran deep in those streets dating back to before he was born. A man didn't survive and live that long and well in this game with too many enemies. That was part of the problem fighting Joe—he had more allies than foes. The only other man that had the power to go against Joe was out of the game.

*****

Spud had truly "made it" by all means of the phrase. Over the years, in the early eighties, it was rumored he made millions and went undetected. He was never flashy, and that truly preserved him. Spud's downfall was a bar fight with a well-known Newark cop, and the cop ended up being shot in front of witnesses. Due to Spud's power and influence at that time, no one would testify against him, but he still got time for the gun. He was famous for attempted murder on a cop and still walked the streets. The judge gave him the maximum on the gun which was five years, but he came home to all the money he had saved and made over the years.

Spud now lived a quiet life. He owned a bike shop in the neighborhood and employed troubled youth. Spud and Trey's uncle, Ali, ran together back in the eighties. Ali went down for a body, and Spud always looked out for his baby sister, Towana, and her only son, Trey.

*****

Trey and Quan had a meeting with a real estate agent. They were planning to buy some property, mostly vacant lots. Their only obligation would have been to fence the property in to keep trespassers out and from getting hurt. They would have them cleaned and paved and just wait. The city's developers would eventually come along and make offers for the property so that they could place new houses on the sites and resell. It was an age-old financial strategy that many Chapter 11 execs had used to their advantage to drain the city's resources and endure financially.

"Look here, dog, we gotta strategize because it's about to get serious," Trey dreaded. "But for now, we have to meet with the real estate agent to see what he talking about," he added before Quan could interject. Trey walked off without looking back.

*****

Joe slammed his fist against the park bench as he clenched his teeth and slit his eyes. Most of his more important men were there, listening to every word. "I want everything around these bastards to fall," Joe ordered. "Anything and everything, with the exception of they momma's and Niki." Joe stayed silent for a few seconds to ensure that his words were understood. His men could imagine why the boys' mothers were off-limits.

Joe knew all the women from the neighborhood. He even went to school with them. Although this was war, there had to be rules; for without rules lurked chaos. Joe also knew that his men would not understand why Niki was off-limits so he offered a brief explanation. "Cheryl not being here with me right now is a feeling I wouldn't wish on my worst enemy." He continued, "And he loves that girl."

The men all looked at each other with anticipation and excitement. Their life's work was proving themselves to Joe in one way or another. Since Joe was loved so dearly in the community, there were few that opposed him so this was truly a rare opportunity. One thing was for sure—there would be bloodshed, and it would go on until Joe was satisfied.

*****

Niki wrapped her hair in a silk scarf that Trey had given her one night as they walked the boardwalk in Atlantic City. As she wrapped her hair, she thought of him constantly. Growing up, even if Trey seemed so outgoing and popular, he was always Niki's teddy bear. He listened carefully and spoke constructively to her. He always seemed to be around. Trey was embedded in Niki's heart and life more than he would ever know. Niki never had the chance to experience another man or even a boy during their childhood. Even when she and Trey were just close friends, his presence was enough to fend off any would-be boyfriends or admirers and that was quite fine with Niki. Trey represented security, peace, success, and love for her. He was truly all that she needed in a man. Since she never knew her father, subconsciously she drew closer to her love for him. She clenched the scarf tighter.

The phone ringing cut into Niki's thoughts as she glanced at the caller ID. It was her mother. Although she loved her mother, she didn't feel much up to talking. Niki was just bathing in thoughts of happiness and the future of her and Trey.

*****

Trey and Quan sat at the light with their thoughts divided as music spilled out the car into the ghetto streets. The meeting had gone well, and they were one step closer to becoming richer. Everywhere they went, attention was focused on them for some reason or another, and Quan loved it. Before they could pull off, out of the corner of his eye, Quan noticed a black Lincoln coming up on the side of them. He quickly reached under the seat for his gun as he urged Trey to pull off.

"Yo, dog, it's a drop!" he yelled while gripping the gun.

Trey realized the attempt to box them in and immediately pulled out in traffic while steering and ducking in the seats. Shots rang out and broke the monotony as bystanders began their scramble to secure their lives.

Quan tried to get a good angle on the Lincoln to shoot back but his attempts proved fruitless as a Cadillac came from the opposite direction, spitting automatic fire at them. There was no doubt in their mind Joe had decided to strike back for Cheryl.

The timing proved detrimental for the two young men. Their only hope lay within Trey's ability to outdrive the older men in his foreign vehicle. As the precious seconds passed by, Trey and Quan finally began to exhale as they realized the two American vehicles had disappeared in the rearview mirror. Neither man spoke as the seriousness of the situation set in.

Trey silently considered seeking Spud's assistance again. Quan sat still, holding his gun that he never used during the whole ordeal. Trey felt a little in over his head while Quan had the taste of war in his mouth. He wanted Joe desperately but tried hard to keep an even head so that he could formulate an effective plan. He flipped open his phone to call Ab and Dee. It was time to bring all the soldiers together on this one. Joe had wasted no time trying to retaliate. He went straight for the gold pot. Quan hung up his phone and shook his head in anticipation. He stared off blankly as he envisioned revenge.

*****

"How in the fuck did you miss?" yelled Joe. To his surprise, he received a phone call that his two favorite enemies were driving carelessly right in front of one of his most reliable men. Joe felt like Christmas had come early. He now reasoned with himself; although he knew he would win, he doubted it would be easy. "You mean to tell me you didn't hit either of these two bastards in broad daylight between the six of you?" he continued, his anger seething through the receiver.

"Boss, somehow they sensed us and pulled off." The man was scared to death as he continued with minimal pause. "The stinking Lincoln was no match for that BMW, boss."

Joe hung up without continuing his verbal assault. His better judgment told him to target the strongest link of their crew, Ab. Joe instantly decided that he would continue to attack the boys' supplier and destroy their army. This double-sided attack would prove too much to sustain. All of the so-called businesses the boys had were just drug fronts, so if he cut off the drug supply, the businesses would wither and die. Or so Joe thought. Joe smiled victoriously at what he was thinking. He grabbed his coat and hurried to his car to propel his plan in action.

*****

"Honey, the meeting went well, but we gon need to go down to DC to finalize things."

Niki looked puzzled as Trey's words penetrated through the phone. It didn't sound logical, but she had no reason to doubt him. "Well, okay, honey, but introduce me as the closing officer. I'll oversee the deals and impose a three percent closing." Niki's business perspective kicked in.

Trey nodded and verbally agreed, knowing he would end up paying Niki out of pocket through one of his other companies.

"How long you gon be gone, baby?" Niki asked, slowly dreading the thought of being without Trey.

"Maybe a couple days," Trey responded as he looked at Quan for a nod of approval. "Yeah baby, a couple days." Trey needed the time to keep Joe occupied and away from Niki. Little did she know within the hour he would call back and ask that she go to DC instead of him, due to a deal that he had "forgotten" and needed to stay local for.

*****

Joe pulled up in front of the brick building that time and poor maintenance had taken advantage of. His army was in place before his arrival, and other members tailed him closely. Joe watched the porch for a few seconds and got out of the car. Minutes later, he sat in a cozy apartment with ice-cream and coffee on the table in front of him. "Sorry about your loss, Joe, I know she meant so much to you." The beautiful woman's voice blanketed the pain Joe brought with him.

Joe searched the room for a comfortable spot to rest his gaze. He had succeeded in a picture of Niki as a young girl. Joe walked over to the picture with a delayed response to Trina's sympathy. "Thanks, Tee." He picked up the picture and stared silently before reaching into his pocket and pulling out a large amount of money and placing it on the table.

"I'm fine, Joe." Trina attempted to explain but was hushed by Joe's hand.

"It's the least, you know…considering." Joe sat and finished his coffee and ice-cream with a smile on his face and a lump in his throat. Trina knew Joe well enough to accept defeat.

"Thanks, Joe." She sat next to Joe and sipped her cup as she watched him. Before long, old stories and laughter took control as the two friends caught up.

"You raised a good kid, Tee," Joe abruptly switched topics.

"Joe, we raised a good kid," Trina offered.

Joe continued as if she hadn't spoken. "Too good to be running around with a street thug that doesn't amount to half of her worth."

Trina stared at Joe and smiled. "She's grown. And besides, he cares for her." She watched Joe for a response as she continued, "He loves her."

Joe stood up and nodded. "Take care, Tee." As quickly as he had come, he left. After all these years, Trina still hadn't felt too fond of Trey but truly questioned her daughter's success without him. It was rumored everywhere that Trey and Quan had been behind most of the drugs and countless murders and violence in the neighborhood, but somehow she couldn't get through to Niki. She tried relentlessly to talk to her daughter but gave up in fear of pushing her away. Trina wasn't willing to risk the unnecessary strain on their relationship. Besides, Niki was happy and successful. She just questioned whether the life of a hustler's woman was something she should accept for her daughter. After all, it hadn't worked for her.

*****

Across town, in his favorite hotel room, Quan lay across the bed watching his latest conquest make her way out of her clothes. The anticipation in the room rose as he stroked himself and nodded gently. "Come to Daddy, girl."

The young lady was unsure why she didn't make it to Quan's actual house and ended up in a hotel room. A very nice room she could tell. In record breaking time, Quan lay flat and naked as he enjoyed Leah's oral ability. He made no effort to return the favor once he decided he had enough and wanted to enter her. Quan bent the young vixen over and placed his hands on each side of her waist and plunged in.

Leah was shocked at the lack of care the ladies' man possessed as he stroked wildly and forcefully back and forth in her. She fought back screams as Quan showcased his skill in sex. Sweat fell from his face, across her back, as she begged for more but was unsure if she could withstand. Quan smiled victoriously as he quickened his pace and slapped her ass. This seemed to be enough to do it.

Leah yelled and screamed in pleasure, begging for more. Quan quickly obliged as he imagined how his performance would be perceived by his boys. Like all of his sexual escapades, Quan taped the act so that he could show the video in all their barber shops throughout the city. Oddly enough, as word spread through the streets about Quan's habit of taping and telling, his popularity with the women grew. The two continued on for the next forty minutes until orgasms had calmed each one respectively.

Quan lay on the bed, tired and satisfied, while Leah lay across him stroking his bare chest. She had not even left, and Quan spoke on the phone with another young lady from the area that his time didn't permit him to enjoy as of yet. As insulted as Leah was initially, she convinced herself that more oral sex would bring him to his senses and he would end the conversation. For now, only her ego would suffer to learn she had been wrong. Once the taped played later, her reputation would suffer the same fate.

*****

Trey walked into the barber shop and headed straight to the back room. The room grew quiet as he passed through with his head toward the floor and Ab closely behind. Just previously, at least thirty men had gone into the same room. All the laughter and chattering ceased as Trey and Ab entered.

"Everybody, we all here on life and death terms," Trey immediately began speaking, looking at no one in particular. "We got everybody to look out for now, from cops to taxi cab drivers, all the way to judges." He continued on while his face wore seriousness and anger.

"If a muthafucka look at anybody from my team wrong, I want him gone." For the first time since entering, Trey looked up and throughout the room to visually check attendance.

Trey had hustler's sectioned and divided throughout the city, performing different duties and tasks with one goal: making money. All of the men shared some of the same traits. They were young, dangerous, and had money. In addition to these qualities, they all had Trey and Quan to thank for their success. Without the two of them, most of these men would have taken on some form of statistic. Their dedication was deadly and precise. The appreciation for the situation gathered control in the room.

Usually, it was Quan who delivered news of this sort, right before or after a viewing of one of his women or more. Trey usually delivered financial strategy and other information pertaining to their wealth and continued success. Ab paced the floor quietly with perfect timing around Trey's words. Everyone in the room knew Ab's reputation and either respected or feared him. He had no children, no particular girl, and was cut off from his family so it appeared as if he had nothing to lose.

As Trey offered advice and direction, his words were interrupted by a cell phone. As everyone fell silent and focused their attention on the owner, Ab stopped suddenly. It was Mel. Mel was in charge of the Southward dope and artillery. He had done well in a short period of time. Operating off instinct, Mel opened up the phone and placed it to his ear. His hello was cut short instantly by three bullets. One to the chest and two head-shots spit from Ab's gun with accuracy. Feet began scrambling in the small room as men began standing and staring in complete shock.

"Did the man not say this was a matter of life and fucking death?" Ab yelled out as he tucked his gun back in. "Any and every fucking thing outside this room don't matter right now. If another phone go off, if a nigga so much as fart to disrupt the wind in here…"

Without finishing his words, Ab looked back at Trey to signal the go head to continue. Simultaneously, heartbeats quickened as cell phones were completely shut off. The words and instructions that followed for the next few minutes caused mayhem and death throughout the city for the next few weeks to come between Trey and Joe, each side losing key players of countless money without an end in sight.

*****

By now, Niki was being penetrated by rumor and gossip that Trey and Quan as well as Joe had a lot to do with the spike in violence in the old neighborhood. Niki was apprehensive about confronting Trey, but she watched him closely. It didn't seem likely or possible. He had no time to do anything else, let alone anything illegal, considering all the time they spent together and his business obligations. She checked the books behind his accountants so his hard work proved beneficial in his finances. She allowed herself to become truly convinced Trey had no time or motive to engage in any illegal activities. Even the time she spent with Quan, as close as they were, she probed in confidence. "Quannie, if something were going on, you would tell me, right?" She looked him seriously in the eye.

Quan returned the look and would reply, "He has too much to lose, sis." With that, she was convinced, despite the body count rising in the streets.

*****

During this war with Joe, Trey tried consistently to have his mother move out of the neighborhood. He was terrified for her and Niki. Niki only went down occasionally to visit her mother which was frightening for Trey, because word had it Joe still stopped by and visited quite often after all these years. Trey feared the worse with Joe catching Niki and harming her. He couldn't imagine living without her, especially if it were his fault he hurt Niki. He constantly battled that thought and, just as easily, pushed it out of his mind.

Quan continued with his routine with the women despite the tension that constantly bubbled throughout the rival crews. Just last week, he had to have a young woman pistol whipped. Turns out she had a live-in boyfriend who threatened her life once word of the tape surfaced in the neighborhood. The next morning, after their escapade, she realized what she had done and begged and pleaded with Quan not to expose her. Quan disregarded it politely until she angered him by constantly asking. Quan opened the hotel room's balcony sliding doors and threw both her clothes and pocketbook down in the parking lot from the second story window. The young lady quickly wrapped herself in the bed spread and hustled toward the door, but just before she could open it and run out, Quan snatched the cover from her. Naked body exposed and in shock, she was then pushed in the hallway and the door was slammed shut immediately as guests in the hallway passed by laughing and pointing.

The hotel's security was forced to call the police for the disturbance. In fear of upsetting Quan or losing his business, the young lady was reported for her obscenity and removed from the premises. She was forced to call her boyfriend from the police station and explain, in addition to asking for clothes. The tape played all over town and didn't make matters any better. He threatened her life, and in turn, she threatened to go to the police on Quan about one of the murders she knew to be his handiwork. She was pistol whipped severely by Ab at the instruction of Quan. The boyfriend mysteriously disappeared. "Two birds with one stone," Quan referred to it.

Trey was worried that Quan had become careless and destructive. He hadn't yet confronted Quan with it but feared the worst.

*****

One day, Trey and Niki walked through the mall, carefree and happily shopping. He had bags in both hands and a smile on his face. Today's shopping spree was Niki's treat. Business had been thriving and their relationship was reaching all time happiness. They strolled past the ice-cream parlor, and Niki gave Trey the look that he couldn't resist.

"No, I know what you thinking." Trey read the look and answered in advance.

"Baby, it's either ice cream or ice." Niki turned and nodded toward a jeweler. She looked back at Trey and leaned in closer. "A vanilla cone is all I want." She spoke softly and seductively, awaiting his reply.

Trey looked at Niki and softly replied, "I'll go for the ice." He walked off briskly toward the jewelry store, satisfied that he had rejected her. He noticed that he didn't hear her footsteps in the distance as he kept moving. Trey convinced himself that if he just kept toward the jeweler, Niki would follow; but he felt her standing there, staring at the back of his head. He didn't budge. He walked into the jewelry store, right up to the counter, pretending not to care.

As he neared the counter, the young lady behind the counter came over and greeted him pleasantly. "Sir, if I may." She held out her hand for Trey's hand, and he could hear Niki behind him walking up. Trey cautiously placed his hand in the girl's hand and quickly but gently, she placed a four carat ring on it as she looked past him at Niki and smiled.

"Something like ice cream I know my man well enough to know he'll say no to," Niki spoke softly in Trey's ear. "Me asking for this hand right here and only this hand for the rest of my days, I can't calculate a no from you."

Trey stood astonished and paralyzed with happiness. "Are you asking what I think you asking?" He stood there, admiring the ring.

"I am." Niki smiled nervously.

Trey quickly responded, "I hope you calculated me saying yes and ready to do this right here and now." The staff of the store broke out in cheers and clapped, capturing the attention of other shoppers both in and out of the store. Trey pulled Niki close and closed his eyes gently as he hugged her. Within that very moment, he knew that somehow, some way, he had to change. Being a husband, someday a father, didn't go too well with cops, gangsters, drugs, and violence. The choice was easy, but the transition would prove anything but.

The day had taken an unexpected upward turn with the proposal. Trey caught himself staring at the ring attentively a few times. Niki had planned the whole day. He didn't see it coming at all. He turned to her, and she seemed to be happier than he. "Baby, let's pick you out a ring," said Trey as he realized that her fingers were bare.

Niki smiled and shook her head no. "Honey, this is a duet, not a duel."

Trey felt a little defeated and quickly gathered his argument, ready for delivery. Then Niki grabbed both his hands and spoke, "You buy a ring when the moment is right, and not a moment before." Wrapping her arms around him, Niki continued. "And honey, you're not smart enough to know when the moment is right. That's what your heart is for. Just listen."

Trey stared at Niki as her words made perfect sense to him. Many men had fallen at the word of Trey's instruction and even his actions—decisions made to kill, ruin, and destroy life, families—and order became a part of his everyday duties, most of the time without even flinching. Somehow, something had to change. It became immediately important to Trey to be a great husband.

*****

Quan pulled his pants up as he removed the condom and threw it on the young lady that lay in the bed. "Oh, hell no, what the fuck is your problem nigga?" She quickly got up and veered toward Quan.

"Fuck you, kiss my ass, suck my dick," was his vicious reply as he dressed. Quan grabbed his hidden camera and made his way out the door with the female yelling obscenities and threats behind him. Within minutes, he was in his car making his way through the streets. Lately, Quan had become more reckless. His focus appeared nonexistent. There was no goal ahead of him. Quan had more money than the average man his age could spend. His power and reputation exceeded him in the streets. He had enough property to start his own village. Women constantly threw themselves at him. The only problem he could even mentally register was this beef with Joe. Many of their barber shops and salons were targets of deadly hits as customers were getting serviced. Men would come in without notice or warning and open fire and leave nothing or no one standing, with the exception of women and children.

Trey and Quan had a hard time keeping up in retaliating. Behind the murders, Joe would send in his crooked cops to investigate and put pressure on the front men of these establishments. Joe hoped he could get one of the men to give Quan and Trey up so if he couldn't get them in the streets, he could at least put them behind bars. Fortunately for Trey and Quan, the people who ran the shops never had enough info on either of them to offer to the police. For this reason, they couldn't cooperate even if they wanted to. Aside from that, Ab was murdering at an alarming rate. A few of the hits were without Quan or Trey's authority, but at this point, his judgment brought them both peace and sanity.

In addition to his dedication and hard work for the boys, he kept a close eye on Niki. Ab knew how important she was to both Trey and Quan, so it was an honor. Dee, on the other hand, had been thinking of getting out. This life didn't seem right for him lately, and it was only a matter of time before he would end up a ghetto statistic—dead or in jail. He carried his duties out with little to no enthusiasm, and it showed to Ab. He took it upon himself to keep a close watch on Dee. He wouldn't report anything until he felt he would have to kill Dee. It seemed drastic, but Ab was truly a soldier and was not able to tolerate a shred of disloyalty. It would be a hard pill to sell to Trey and Quan without sufficient proof.

*****

Niki sat back with her wine grasped in her hand as her mind floated to a future. A future decorated with Trey, a beautiful home, and two children. It was likely they'd have to purchase two separate dogs, because he was such an aggressive person while she was dainty and polite, and their respective dogs would reflect their personalities. She mentally went over all the details, and an excitement began building slowly but surely.

Although Niki miraculously overcame her circumstance, she was not able to escape the stigma of coming from a broken home. Niki never knew who her father was, and although she and her mom were super close, it was a piece of the puzzle that could not be overlooked. A few years prior, she had made a fool of herself in thinking Spud was her father. So many things added up to her that gave her the sense of security to confront him. He had proven to be such a gentleman in letting her down easy and confirming that although he had always an interest in Trina, he was not afforded the opportunity to offer her a child as great as Niki. She didn't want this life for her children. They would be a perfect nuclear family in all its splendor and glory. Niki's wine, infused with her thoughts, delivered her into a peaceful sleep in the comfort of her beautiful home.

*****

Ab finalized his prayer in the comfort of his home as he hurried his pace so that he would catch Dee leaving his house, which was not too far away. He had noticed many indications that Dee's heart wasn't in his work and that his mind wasn't on the job lately. Mistakes of the wrong caliber would cost everyone everything, with or without their consent in their line of work. Ab was not in a position to allow someone else's weakness to serve him to failure. Too much was at stake. Moments later, he neared the corner just in time to catch Dee exiting the bodega. His sights were locked on his target who carried a sandwich in one hand and his cell phone in another. Ab wished that he were close enough to hear Dee's end of the conversation without being noticed. He hoped he'd find reason to conclude his dear friend's life or at least reinvest his trust in him. For everyone's sake, it was desperately needed.

*****

Trey and Quan embraced each other with a heartfelt hug as Quan smiled and exclaimed, "Sis got my nigga to settle all the way down." Trey just nodded in agreement as he unlocked their embrace to greet a few guests arriving in the upscale restaurant.

"Over here, Ms. Trina," as he motioned to Niki's mom and a few of her friends. It was their engagement dinner, and the moment was priceless. Against his better judgment, Trey did not invite Ab and Dee. He was certain that Joe would follow them if it were obvious both his head muscle guys were at the same place at the same time.

All the men that were there to protect them this evening were from out of town. That way, if anything occurred, there would be nothing but rumor and speculation on the grapevine, nothing that would actually lead back to either of them.

Trey walked over to Trina and grabbed her hand gently as he led her away from the crowd to a room just before the restroom. Trina followed with a slight reluctance. Just as quickly as he could get Trina in the room, he closed the door and began speaking. "Your baby is my lady." Trey held Trina's hand and spoke passionately. "I want to be the beginning of her forever and the end of her search for love." Trina smiled and fought back tears as she listened with great anticipation for the next word. "My life didn't begin until she became mine," Trey continued. "I need to have your blessing in order for this to be complete."

Trey didn't move and almost held his breath, waiting for her to reply. Although Niki had no father, he understood how close she and her mother were as well as how much it would mean if she was on board. "Trey, she asked you. My baby, my lovely daughter, came to me and she spoke of how she felt and what she needed, and every sentence ended with your name." Trina rubbed Trey's head and smiled. "This is the only way she'll be happy, and I'm happy and I trust you. I trust you with her life."

The room was filled with joy and relief as they smiled at one another. Laughter erupted back in the main room, followed by cheers, and they both knew that was Niki making her grand entrance.

Luxurious curls rested on Niki's shoulders, kissing her bare skin in a silver open-back dress that was topped off with perfect diamond earrings and silver shoes. Her smile seemed to be a melody in itself as she graciously swept the room, greeting guests. In that moment, she gave Trey the perfect mental picture of what a perfect bride she would be.

Everyone ate and laughed as Quan narrated stories of the couple that kept everyone entertained. There was no sign of violence as if there was a truce for the evening. For the first time in a long time, Trey was able to exhale. It felt good. His queen at his side, his friend and brother, Quan, was on his best behavior. There was no gunfire, no screams of terror, no money being exchanged, or deals on the table. Life was good.

*****

Joe's men sat idle and anxious, wondering why if Quan and Trey were together and Ab and Dee were not there, they weren't attacking. This could be the end all be all to the back and forth. There was unrest due to some of the high-ranking members of Joe's crew taken out by Trey and Quan. No one wanted to be next. Some of these men had served for twenty years or more. It was outright insulting to be taken out by some new age street punks. Despite the unrest, all the men knew better to challenge Joe's discretion on any issue.

Joe lay in a recliner in his office, holding a graduation picture of Niki. He stared for hours and hated the way his life was structured. He wasn't able to come forth in being Niki's father because of a beef he had with Spud at the time. He and Trina had been seeing each other, but it had also been said she was seeing Spud as well. Trina didn't know that Joe was aware of the rumor.

Joe wasn't able to trade in a life of women, cars, travel, violence, and notoriety to stay home and live such a mundane life. He always thought the life he led would make Trina and Niki an easy target. He thought it better to be discreet but provide financial support. Trina hated the idea but agreed out of fear for her safety. Although Spud had been interested when they were young, she knew it would be the ultimate disrespect to Joe to be with Spud. Nothing ever became of it, despite an undeniable attraction.

*****

A few days had passed, and Trey had spent more time in his legitimate business ventures than in the drug trade that he cultivated. Mentally, he prepared himself for the life of a husband, and although he didn't exactly plan to retire, he knew the two lifestyles would not go hand in hand. It was a conflict that he had to acknowledge. Aside from that, his absence may have kept Joe at bay.

Quan was back to his escapades, and Ab was getting restless. The quietness was generating an inner anxiety in him. Dee, on the other hand, was acclimating himself to a new way of life.

Breakfast lay across the kitchen table while Dee exited the bedroom to make his way down to devour his share. The kids had gone off to school so it was just he and Leslie. She was overdressed for the occasion, in his opinion, as he eyeballed her, then the food, and then again at her. His plan of action was to start with the food and then onto her. Leslie could feel him sizing her up as she prepared his plate. They both smiled, anticipating what lay ahead for each of them respectively.

The doorbell cut into a devilish grin and a light sigh. Since Leslie was preparing food, Dee hurried to the door with agitation in his tone as he yelled, "Who's there?" Before he got a response, he had the door opened, and Ab stood in the doorway blocking the sun's invasion.

"See, you supposed to figure out who it is before you let the nigga in," Ab snarled as he bullied his way in. He turned and moved in an uncomfortably close distance to Dee. "Get dressed nigga, get yo heat too." Dee didn't respond. He tried to manufacture a false interest, but the tension was noticeable between the two soldiers. Dee turned and traveled to the kitchen to grab his plate to go. Leslie was used to it. She made no effort to conceal her disappointment while offering Ab some food. Ab declined in a respectful manner as he stood holding his hat out of respect for the lady's presence, Shortly after, Dee was ready to embark on whatever journey lay ahead for the day.

"Everything good, soldier?" Ab asked as he and Dee drove in silence.

"Yeah, bro, why you ask?" Dee replied, feeling the question to be more of an accusation than an actual question.

Ab offered no further explanation. He signaled for Dee to pull over near a crowd of men leaving a neighborhood sandwich shop. Before the vehicle could near the curb, Ab rolled down the window and opened fire in one sweeping motion. Dee brought the car to a complete stop, and Ab jumped out to further his execution. Each

man that scurried was met with shots to the torso to slow their flee-
ing, and an immediate shot to the head to ensure no resistance—six
men in total.

While Ab turned and fired, he noticed one of the men firing
back while attempting to flee. He couldn't approach while firing,
because the man's gun spit bullets angrily in his direction. While the
man focused on taking Ab down in this blaze of glory, he felt the hot
burn of slugs trespassing in his back and shoulder. He turned in the
opposite direction while falling from his wounds. Dee was aiming at
him while his teeth dug into his lips. He was outnumbered and didn't
see a way out of this. The realization fell upon him as he clashed to
the curb. Although he knew what direction Ab was in, he slowly lost
control of his ability to move his limbs and protect himself. He was
a sitting duck.

Ab stared at Dee from over the car and gun smoke. He waited a
few seconds before he moved around the vehicle and stood over the
wounded man. He aimed his gun for the man's head while he stared
at Dee. He locked eyes and, without emotion, squeezed three times.
Dee struggled not to turn away but refused to look at the dead man.
A few seconds passed as Ab still stared Dee. The awkwardness settled
quickly. Dee struggled to make eye contact with Ab. Thankfully, he
didn't have to as Ab turned suddenly and ran toward the car.

The two men raced away from the scene as Ab calmly started in
on Dee. "You can't wait to react. You have to be the acting force to set
things in motion." His hand motions corroborated the conviction of
his statement. Dee nodded and began to speak but was interrupted
by Ab with a higher, stronger tone. "Why shoot to wound when the
very man you leave behind will come back and kill you, your lady,
and yo fucking kids, nigga?" Ab turned and locked his eye on Dee as
he drove aggressively.

"Watch the road, dog! Shit, man!" Dee's only reply infuriated
Ab. He refused to show emotion though. As he calmed himself, Dee
began to get more and more nervous. "You didn't even let me know
what was going on, man, how was I supposed to know?" Dee furthered his argument. Ab offered no response. He only drove. Dee
had no idea of what just occurred. He had no clue of why those

men were just killed but assumed it was at Trey and Quan's request. He did recognize it to be one of Joe's spots. He was starting to feel a strange sense of relief due to all the inactivity lately. None of their people had been hit, and they were not being ordered to hit any of Joe's people. He felt like they just set the war back in motion.

Uneasiness crept into his soul as Ab slowed the car down in a close-by suburb. He pulled to the curb and reached into the backseat for two zip lock bags. He sprayed his gun with an ammonia and alcohol mixture and quickly wiped it down. The gun was deposited in the bag and the bag zipped airtight. Dee didn't hesitate in doing the same. This was their routine to ensure guns were not linked to anyone or used twice. They tossed the guns in the sewer and took off.

Ab decided to take the highway back to avoid talking to Dee any more than necessary. Dee's attempts to create small talk were met with all one-word answers. He was either persistent or not intelligent enough to get the point. As quickly as he could turn the radio on, Ab immediately shut it off. He had never been more uncomfortable around his boy. He wasn't sure where the tension was coming from. His ringtone cut the silence open.

Dee's face stretched into a smile once he looked and saw it was Leslie. "Baby, you know I'm working," he answered. There was a pause on the other end followed by a male's voice.

"I am too, young nigga, I'm working too." Muffled sounds of screaming followed by six gun shots were all that could be heard. Dee's heart dropped to his stomach.

"Nooooo!" he yelled. Ab turned and looked with an uninterested expression. He didn't bother asking what the issue was. Despite Dee immediately bursting into tears, Ab expended no concern. His heart was as cold as Christmas eve in Chicago. "Dog, they got Leslie!" Dee's head rested limply in his hands as tears overflowed. "They got her, just that fast."

Ab turned to him and responded slowly with an even toned, "That's the game."

Dee didn't know what to do. He wanted to rush home and make sure the children were safe. They would be home from school soon. He didn't want them to see her. What would he do with two children and no Leslie? His mind raced a mile a minute. "I gotta go home and…and—"

Ab jumped in, "And get fucking killed yourself? That's all that can happen. They got to her that fast being good, nigga, not emotional." He spoke over the sobbing coming from Dee. "That's a skillset that can only be met with a level mind, not crying like no bitch and come running into an ambush."

Dee became instantly angry. He also realized how helpless he was. He knew better than to attempt to attack Ab or he could very well be killed with Ab's bare hands. Joe had won another round. Just when the fight seemed to slow down to almost a halt, a whirlwind of pain coming whirling down. Joe was a chess player in the art of war. He went for the heart of Trey and Quan's muscle men. Little did he know that Ab's heart was buried deep into the game and not in any one human or possession.

*****

Quan entered the funeral home dressed to steal the attention of any young lady who dared to look in his direction. He didn't know Leslie well, but he knew women would fill the place. His cut was groomed perfectly, and cologne seemed to whisper to any lady who came within arm's length. As he surveyed the room of grieving bachelorettes, two twins stuck out. They didn't seem to be as sad as everyone else there, and their identical faces were not familiar. Most of these people were either from the neighborhood, knew him, or he knew them. These two were different. They were exotic looking, and most Newark girls didn't have their features.

Quan was officially stricken. They only chatted amongst themselves and they scanned the wake as if they also knew no one. There was no good time to introduce himself at such a function, but he couldn't let the opportunity pass him by. A face leaned in toward Quan's and broke his gaze on the women. "Hey, bro," Niki softly spoke.

Quan looked up and gathered himself immediately. He kissed Niki's cheek and turned to look for Trey. He spotted him in the distance moving slowly toward the crowd, checking the men's faces out of precaution. Quan hurried around Niki and moved in toward Trey. As he passed seats, he noticed Ab all dressed up amongst the crowd, sitting alone, pretending not to know him. Quan knew Ab well enough to know this was part of his protection plan. He didn't stop until he reached Trey. A quick embrace and two genuine smiles between the two served as the greeting.

"Bro, you see them bitches up front with the yellow on?" Quan started with an apparent excitement.

Trey shook his head and chuckled, "Dog, we at a wake, watch yo mouth."

Quan was slightly embarrassed, but continued on, "You know them?"

Trey studied briefly, shaking his head no. "Can't say I do, they probably Leslie cousins or something. You know everybody got somebody from down south," Trey rationalized. Before he could get another syllable in, Quan was headed toward the front row.

It was good measure to come to the wake and support Dee. He hadn't been himself since Leslie was killed. Aside from all face shots, Joe's men poured an entire bottle of gin on her body and set her on fire. The house nearly burned to ashes. Dee moved the kids to Maryland with her mother and had been staying at Quan's the past week. This was too much for Trey to explain to Niki. He informed her that Leslie stole some money from her ex and he had been looking for her since he'd gotten out and finally caught up with her. He only prayed she didn't get the street's version of events.

Quan slid across the seat next to Dee and put his hand on his shoulder in a calming manner. "Look here, my nigga, I know you going through it and all right now, but I just got one question for you."

Dee looked up, teary eyed and weak, awaiting the question. Quan nodded toward the twins without saying a word. Dee knew Quan well enough to know what he wanted. "Not right now, but I got you, dog," Dee promised.

Quan, unsatisfied with that, pressed on. "Why don't you come introduce me properly and I'll be out your hair?" he counteroffered.

Without putting up any resistance, Dee walked over to the twins and kneeled down. Quan immediately followed with a little distance, not to undermine his cool. As he noticed the twins look around Dee to notice him, he smiled and began moving in. All was not lost. Not a bad day for everyone. Not for Quan at least.

Niki sat and watched the crowd. Tears ran down her face but not for the common reason as everyone else. The amount of men here was overwhelming. She wondered which one could be her father. Secretly, whenever she was in the presence of several black men, she would examine their features. She would ask herself, "Is this him? Could this be my father?" It was a pain that she could never outgrow. She had tried over the years, but the curiosity and pain only came back with vengeance. Trey held her hand and comforted her the best he knew how, although he didn't comprehend why she was so shaken up by Leslie.

Ab scanned the room, poised for action. If one person appeared to pose a threat to Quan, Niki, or Trey, there would be two bodies laying to rest. Or three or four or however many it took. He watched Dee, and although he felt bad for him, he also hoped that Leslie not being around any longer would strengthen his heart. He silently hoped it would provide him with the killer instinct he once possessed. For now, he only felt bad for him. The weakest link had just gotten weaker.

A couple weeks had passed, and Trey was missing on most of the day-to-day decisions. He occupied himself with business and learned a valuable lesson. It took time, effort, and consistency to perpetrate that particular fraud. Ironically, it took him away from the streets. Not out of Joe's scope, but out of his immediate sights. Ab stuck close by Trey. He had no interest in learning anything productive while he had several opportunities to do so. He only wanted to protect his dear friend. His loyalty could never be questioned.

By default, Dee spent more time with Quan. He would frequently be caught gazing into nowhere and tearing up. The loss of Leslie was more than he anticipated. It was far more than he could bare. He had no reasonable chance of ever recovering. Speaking to the children on the phone only made things worse. He had no answer for the questions they asked. He felt responsible, and deep down inside, he knew that he was. Although he couldn't save her, he at least wanted to be the first person on the scene to find her. Not some stranger that didn't know her and didn't love her. There were so many things he wished he had done differently.

Quan had been speaking back and forth with the twins. They were from Florida and flew out the next morning after Leslie's funeral. He had offered several times to fly them back out to New Jersey so they could spend some time together. Their schedules hadn't permitted as of yet. Meanwhile, the acquaintance grew stronger by text and phone conversations. He had a few ladies to keep him occupied until he got what he really wanted, though.

All the dope from Trey and Quan's operation had to now be sold out of apartment buildings. Anyone standing on corners was shot and killed within the hour. It was difficult recruiting new help, because everyone knew they would be walking into the middle of a war. It was even more difficult for Joe to acquire new help. His guys were older, had been operating for years, and were quite the contrast to the pant-sagging, tattoo-bearing, foreign car driving, rap music listening young men on Trey and Quan's roster. These were grandfathers in most cases, not at all to be taken lightly, though. Despite the tailor-made suits, Italian loafers, and late model Cadillacs, some of these guys had been to jail for ten and twenty years and never opened their mouths; stand-up guys all around the board.

In response to being run in the buildings, Trey and Quan ordered any of the fiends that they knew who were buying from Joe to be shot and killed. This tactic evoked so much fear in his loyal customers; if they didn't switch over to them, they were going into rehabs altogether.

A long day pressed Quan to retire back into the comfort of his condo. He multitasked between fumbling through his phone for a qualified young female to entertain and driving home. He knew that Dee was a few cars behind to keep an eye out. Lately, he and Trey had not been carrying firearms in fear of getting pulled over and arrested. They relied totally on their counterparts for protection.

Dee had practically been staying with Quan since Leslie was killed. As he neared his condo community, he doubled the block twice, quickly scanning the cars parked outside and the faces inside. Dee would usually go straight upstairs to guarantee no one was lurking. Quan was just finalizing his conversation with the twins, pulling into the parking spot. Dee was calling on the other line. "Yo, what up?" he softly spoke into the phone.

"You need to get up here, shit ain't right," Dee spat back. Quan's mood entirely changed as he hurried his pace upstairs. He had instantly made up his mind to move before the month was out.

As he entered the home, he could tell someone had been there. The place wasn't a wreck, but things were out of place. Dee emerged from one of the bedrooms with his weapon drawn. "It's all good now, but check this out," he advised as he motioned for Quan to follow him.

He took Quan to the bedroom where there were condoms all over the bed, more condoms than he had seen in one place at one time. Both men stood over the bed, shaking their head in disbelief. Quan began moving around the room and checking inventory. The situation just got more complex. The only thing Quan was missing was DVDs. Every escapade that he'd ever taped was missing out of his library. He kept it in a secret compartment in his closet. He assumed only his boys knew where he kept it, but it could have been some chick that caught him slipping one night she stayed over. He slowly relaxed as he rationalized that this was the work of an overzealous woman. It had to be. Maybe this wasn't so bad after all. He lay down on the bed smirking as Dee stood over him looking puzzled. "All's well my nigga, all's well," he chuckled.

*****

Trey stuffed the clothes he loved to see Niki in best in a suitcase laying on the bed as she showered. He had convinced her to go to Delaware for an investment opportunity. She didn't see the purpose of going without him but complied as a good business partner, fiancé, and wife-to-be. Trey stepped back and looked at his handiwork and shook his head. He packed all dresses, no panties or bra, and two pair of pants. Seemed like a good idea as he packed, but he knew she'd come in and revamp his system. Niki exited the shower with her hair wrapped in one towel and her body in a separate one. She moved closer toward the suitcase, wondering what Trey thought he was doing. "Baby, are you serious?" she spoke softly in a loving manner.

Before she could utter another word, her admirer closed in and placed his face as close to hers a possible. As soon as he made eye contact, he kissed her while undoing her towel. There were no words as important as the action about to take place. Trey lifted Niki up and used his foot to shove the suitcase off the bed. He gently placed her on the bed and began strategically placing kisses all over her body. Soft moans and supple kisses provided the room's melody as he continued. She smelled so good, he couldn't help but inhale as he kissed. Afraid to forget a spot, he started back down at her feet, caressing and placing soft kisses. As he moved upward on her legs, he incorporated tongue. His hands roam her body all the while.

Niki's anxiety took precedence as she sat up and pulled Trey closer. He could read her body language but decided he was the orator in this conversation. He teased her more with the sensual massage of his tongue and hands simultaneously. Her pace and breathing raced to ecstasy while her tour guide took the scenic route. His mouth touched her clitoris, and she nearly sat up erect. Her response heightened the moment for him. He wrestled her clitoris with his tongue and massaged her legs. She panted and jerked while struggling to lie still. This torture filled with pleasure and delight was an emotional and mental paradise. She didn't want to visit; Niki wanted to become a native. The tongue here was persuasive and demanding. She would gladly submit to this type of ruling.

Trey was relentless in his pursuit of satisfaction. There was no mercy in his execution. He came up for air only long enough to kiss her and taunt her with his finger. The moisture had turned into a small stream of anticipation and excitement. Her hopes of controlling the situation were dilapidating quickly. Niki's breasts were the next focus point of pleasure. He cupped them with his mouth while never letting his hands become idle. There was said to be a fine line between making love and fucking. The lines were erased and the art of two museums combined and were on display in their bedroom. The mood heightened by the minute, which only offered more motivation to deliver ample attention to hidden areas.

Niki's hands wandered until she found something to hold onto. Something long, hard, and stable to hold onto. As she held Trey in her hand, while he grazed on her breast, she climaxed. Her body went into simple convulsions as the orgasm took place. There was no turning back now. Trey opened her legs and inserted himself while she still lay shaking and panting. She sat up and clinched him tightly with her hands wrapped around his back. Trey kissed his wife-to-be passionately the entire time he was within her safety. His lips never left hers. His hands never touched the bed, only her body which he worshipped as his personal temple. Suddenly, packing was not as important.

An hour transformed into an eternity lying in Trey's arms. They were submerged in a love so deep that suffocation was a better option than coming up for air. Love set their friendship on fire, and their relationship was engulfed in flames. "Tell me about your wedding day," said Trey as he broke the silence. Niki hesitated momentarily. Without words being offered, Trey knew what the hesitation was for. "I call it your day, because it's the day everyone in our world will see you the way I see you."

Niki smiled and Trey continued, "It's your day because my only job is to show up and claim my life's prize."

Tears emerged from Niki's eyes as she forced words to the surface. "I won't have a daddy to give me away." Niki uttered the words as if she were at her own wake. The words cut the mood open, and pain spilled out.

Trey sat up while holding Niki's head. "Baby, it's gon be all right, family is who we connect and share our love with the most in life." He moved her hair away from her face and kissed a single tear.

Niki slightly moved away as she firmly asserted, "Yeah, but a father is irreplaceable." The embrace was broken, and suddenly she was packing while the tears flowed endlessly. Trey sat on the bed with a feeling of helplessness. The thought of who would give Niki away at their wedding never occurred to him. He had no expectation of what actually took place at weddings. She was his only focus.

*****

Dee walked into a dimly lit bedroom in Quan's house, handing him the phone. Quan was laid back as a young lady provided him oral pleasure. "Bro, the twins on the phone," he announced while handing Dee the phone. Quan barely moved as he reached up for the phone. He took notice that the phone that was being handed to him was Dee's cell phone. For a brief second, he wondered why they wouldn't have just called his phone. Suspicion and paranoia were bullying Quan's thoughts lately with all that had been going on. He answered, offering a slight moan of pleasure, which motivated the young lady more. The conversation was quick and beneficial. They would be coming into town and wanted to hook up. Quan laid his head back and allowed himself to be coerced into sexual bliss, all the while thinking of his next encounter with the twins.

*****

Trina had been pleading with Joe to stop the war. She saw an inevitable loss ahead for Niki. Either her father or her husband-to-be would be gone from her life forever. Joe's pride and ego wove an iron-clad drive to keep going, despite her pleas. He looked at this situation entirely different as between he and Trey being who they were. Niki was the only one safe in this entire war. She was truly the only person that was off-limits for everyone on both sides.

A certain pain came into play knowing that he had such a wonderful, beautiful daughter that he couldn't indulge in. He often rationalized that it was best because of the life he lived. In his mind, she was better off without him. If only he knew. The news of Niki and Trey's engagement gave Joe mixed feelings. He didn't want that life for his daughter. If he had stayed away from her based on his lifestyle, he couldn't, in good conscience, offer her to a younger version of himself. He also wondered if he had let this occur, would Trey move Niki away and retire altogether? That was highly unlikely in Joe's mind as he knew from firsthand experience once hustling was in your blood, it didn't go away unless your blood dried up.

Joe wasn't able to turn back if he wanted to as he had instilled the incentive to kill in fifty men across the city. It was truly too late to turn back, and Trina just didn't understand that. In fact, this was partly her fault for waiting so long to tell Joe that Niki was his daughter. In fact, to ensure that this war didn't lose momentum, Joe directed one of his guys to go shoot up the barber's shop Quan and Trey frequented. Even if he didn't get them personally, it would affect them nonetheless.

As the only woman exited the barber's shop with her nine-year-old son, Joe's men entered. They waited patiently outside so that no women or children were injured. The barber smiled and nodded as the two older gentleman walked in. The would-be killers took a quick look while asking, "How much is a cut and shave?" Their questions were met with gunfire. The barber's instinct told him the men being groomed properly and shaven already were not there for the kind of business they alluded to. The gunfire didn't cease until the guns were empty. Rapid fire quickly tore through suits, flesh, and bone to mow down the assassins. There could be no room for error or retaliation. Just as the guns emptied, the barber moved to the door to look outside to make sure a second round of shooters were not waiting in the wing. Once he was satisfied the coast was clear, he went to his cabinet and took out kerosene and poured it over the dead men and also made a trail throughout the barber's shop. He grabbed his coat, lit a match, and walked out. Smoothly, calmly walking to his car, he wiped down his gun and placed it in a zip lock bag. The man started his car and made his way to a suburban sewer.

*****

Ab was busy with every option of taking human life. A few days prior, he was convinced that the car in front of him was Joe in traffic. The driver was paying attention to the road more than its driver's, and Ab had to capitalize on the moment. It was a nice day so the driver had his window rolled down, enjoying the music. Ab knew that the back windows where Joe sat would likely be bulletproof so once the driver pulled up to the light, he made his move. He pulled alongside the driver and aimed his weapon. His high-caliber handgun removed a majority of the man's head before he could even realize what was happening. For the finishing touches, Ab threw a hand grenade in and pulled off. Even if the windows were bulletproof, the entire vehicle would be blown away and the protected passenger would be blown to smithereens. He pulled off immediately and followed the routine for weapon disposal. He was satisfied. He couldn't confirm it was Joe, but the sound of the explosion in the background offered him joy all the same.

Chaos ran rampant in the city as bodies piled from both sides in a war that would have no winners. The reason was unclear, but the participants were equally devoted. The police were focusing more and more genuine efforts to find some of the killers, and residents were afraid for the very lives. Every killing was a result of strategy and planning from careful men in the craft so the police really had their work cut out for them. The police that Joe had on payroll were almost obsolete as the mayor was now involved. More pressure than ever was on to make valid arrests, but that didn't deter anyone.

Darkness lay a still blanket over a deadly city while a young, handsome Quan adjusted his tie in the mirror. The best of Luther Vandross carried the mood of the house from upbeat dance tempos to soothing love ballads. Quan had become overwhelmed with thoughts of monogamy lately. "Could a man settle down with two women?" he asked himself seriously. He hadn't any exposure to women who spoke well, had no interest in the club scene, and was not impressed by who he was. It was a refreshing contrast to what he was accustomed to.

The twins were not concerned with his reputation, and that intrigued him. He had an elaborate date planned ahead. It included romance, infused by an obvious chemistry, attraction, and high levels of sexual anticipation. He stared in the mirror until he was satisfied with his finishing touches. A lot of planning went into tonight's festivities. Quan had asked Dee to leave for the next few days. Since Leslie died, he had been there moping, reminiscing, and on some late nights he could even hear him sobbing in a neighboring bedroom. This really did undermine his ability to be a valid source of protection as far as Quan was concerned.

The doorbell cut into Luther's perfectly pitched notes. Quan closed his eyes and exhaled. An unfamiliar nervousness engulfed him as he turned to make way to the buzzer. "Who's there?" he asked, as if he didn't know.

"Ashley," spoke one twin.

"Aaliyah," followed another.

The sound of the buzzer to allow entrance was the next thing that could be heard. He hurried through the house to light the vanilla candles and rewind the track "If This World Were Mine." There were rose pedals around the edge of the bed as well as in the Jacuzzi, with various bottles of wine on ice and fruit. He cracked the house door and waited for his gift to present themselves.

The door was stretched open, and a flowing white gown kissing the floor followed by a short white dress entered. They looked magnificent. He was truly taken aback by the beauty and poise these women possessed. Although it took two women, Quan felt he was finally equally yoked. This was the first time he didn't feel as if he was more attractive, had more access to financial resources, and more class than a female counter part. One woman carried a bottle of wine while the other had three glasses.

Quan walked smoothly across the marble floor with his lips tucked and his eyes locked. He hugged them both while they placed kisses on opposing sides of his neck. His body tingled. Within seconds, the bottle was opened, and the wine filled the glasses. Each person held a glass and smiled as sips were taken. No words had been spoken as of yet, and the ambiance was so delicate and wild simultaneously. It was almost the equivalent to being at a wedding and on the set of an adult film.

The incentive to kiss overpowered the need to speak as Quan grabbed the back of Aaliyah's head and tasted her tongue as if it were an expensive chocolate. Ashley tilted down Quan's shirt collar and wrote her name on his neck with her tongue. He couldn't help but moan. As a man, Quan was ashamed that he allowed a moan to escape. He quickly shed his shame as he changed from Aaliyah to Ashley. Most of their conversation was spent over long nights and early mornings. The door was still open as Quan and the twins engaged. Timing and chemistry didn't offer the opportunity for small civil gestures. This experience was so beautiful, he instantly decided not to record it.

*****

Trey sat in his recliner, staring at Niki's picture and the scarf he had bought her. She usually wrapped her hair in it. She left in such haste that she'd forgotten her scarf. He admired her beauty as if she was another man's woman and he wanted her for himself. It was the first time they'd been apart. Although he knew it was for the best, he didn't like it. Her mood when she left didn't make things better.

Lately, it had occurred to Trey how much not having or knowing her father affected her. It was a situation he couldn't direct or control, and that bothered him. Trey's mother had been arrested for transporting drugs when he was younger. His father was afraid she'd cooperate with the police so he left town without saying a word. Trey's mother was so in love with his father, she accepted responsibility for everything and received a thirty-year sentence. Once she heard that Lee had run out on their only child, she killed herself just a few years into the sentence.

Trey was genuinely unaffected. He assumed that it was the ingredient he needed to be a hardened hustler. He never spoke of it and never showed emotion one way or another. Niki was different. As strong as she was, she was also delicate and incomplete. He hoped his love and dedication to her was enough to complete her.

His phone pierced his thoughts. He looked down, and Niki's profile picture shed light on a dreary mood. "Baby, why you not here with me?" Trey asked as if he didn't know the answer to the question.

"I'll tell you why. Because my husband asked me to do something and so it shall be done!" Niki's response melted Trey's hardened exterior. He had no retort. He smiled from ear to ear, and she continued, "So what's our bottom line on this property? Are we paying an out-of-state commission to buy? Or is there an incentive to sell?" The mood of the conversation was quickly switched to business.

"Do what you want, you are the boss," Trey offered as a response.

"Baby, make sure you eat properly, and I left something for you in the nightstand drawer."

Trey got up and started toward the nightstand as Ab walked in. "I'll eat. You just get back here." Ab noticed Trey was on the phone and stood silent. "Niki," Trey waited for a response. "I love you, girl," he blurted as she began to speak.

Tears raced down her face as she ended the call. She had to get back to him as quickly as possible. Trey removed a letter from the nightstand drawer. The look on Ab's face was serious and sincere, so Trey shoved the letter in his pocket as he asked, "What's up, dog?"

"We gon wait on the word, I put some work in and we just waiting to see who it was," Ab calmly explained.

Trey extended a handshake to Ab as he spoke, "It wasn't Joe."

"Word got back already, but it wasn't him." Ab turned angrily and began to leave.

"Nah, I need you, man. I got some moves to make, and I need you by my side."

Ab smiled at Trey. "Do what you do. I'm always by your side, even when you don't know it."

Trey knew he was telling the truth. Ab quickly turned and left as quickly as he had come.

No one knew exactly where Joe lived or even lay his head. Although this was to be expected, it was frustrating to say the least. Ab had been hunting his men and was pleased with his results until lately. He wanted Joe, and nothing else would suffice at this point. He wouldn't be able to live with himself if Joe had gotten to Trey, Niki, or Quan before he could save them. He hoped Dee was equally motivated, but he knew better.

Ab would gather every soldier in their army and offer clear instructions. Joe needed to be killed within the next few days.

Preferably before Niki returned as Ab knew Joe would strike at their wedding. It was a race against time.

*****

Trey tried to keep a low profile as he went from A to B lately in the streets. An all-black Corvette pulled into a parking spot at the mall two towns over. This was considered as low as he could go in terms of transportation. He had yet to place that ring to seal the deal on Niki's hands. With her in town, she'd usually be with him or he'd be working harder than the average man to make the day go by faster until they reconnected.

Before he evacuated the vehicle, he looked at every car around him and at every person in passing. This had become part of his routine more than usual lately. Couldn't be too sure. Trey entered the mall nearest the store he was interested in. He scanned every face in passing while he headed straight to Zales. He walked in the store and sighed a slight sign of relief. He walked over to the rings and stared in the case.

A young woman yelled out, "Sir, I be right with you as soon as I finish with these gentlemen." The two men the lady was helping turned and looked in Trey's direction. The store suddenly became quiet and still. It was Joe. He and his bodyguard were buying watches. All three men hesitated while staring one another down. Joe and his guy walked slowly over to Trey. Although he wasn't armed, he refused to run. If death had led him to this store, the purpose alone was worth his life in his book.

Joe walked up and extended his hand. Trey didn't budge. The man spoke while staring Trey in the face. "Show some fucking respect and address the man as a gentleman would." Joe stood there with his hand extended.

"You got to give respect to get it, old timer," Ab shot back from over Trey's shoulder. Trey had never been happier to hear his friend's voice. His odds were instantly and greatly increased. The sales rep noticed the exchange and was stricken with fear. The tension in the room was thick and barely moved. She preferred to go unnoticed.

49

Ab walked up and stood alongside Trey. "Good afternoon, fellas," he spoke while looking at Joe. Trey now felt the confidence to shake Joe's hand. Joe forced a smile and spoke in a low deep tone.

"I'm not surprised to see you here. You got a wedding to attend, correct?"

Trey nodded for a response.

Joe's bodyguard spoke next, "Better that than a funeral."

Ab stepped in closer and the man reached in his overcoat. Ab looked him in his eye while shaking his head. "Nobody walks out alive if you try that."

The man weighed his options and looked at Joe.

Ab continued, "There is only one guaranteed survivor, and that person would rot in the cell to tell the story how he pleased."

Joe looked at his guy and shook his head. He intervened by speaking to Trey again. "Pick out something elegant, priced more than a Cadillac, but simple and exquisite." He moved around him and began walking out while yelling out, "I hear she's worth it."

Trey turned to Ab without words to express his gratitude. "Get your ring, man." Ab sensed the mood and walked out smiling.

The saleslady's fear had subsided enough to offer Trey assistance in finding Niki a four-karat princess-cut ring. This ring spoke to him as he stared at it. He could envision Niki jumping and screaming as she exclaimed her satisfaction. He smiled at the ring as if it were Niki herself. The jewelry embodied her personality. This was it. Trey made his purchase and hurried to his car.

As he started the car, he noticed a black Mercedes pulling alongside him. He recognized it to be Ab. "I got you, dog, just don't go straight home." Trey's excitement limited his speech. He could only quickly shake his head. In this moment, he was happy. All that he needed in life was to lie with a woman that only wanted him and to contribute to making him a better man. He wanted to call Niki, just to talk, but didn't want to risk making Ab's job harder by not paying attention. *Besides, she was probably busy handling business*, he reasoned.

*****

Joe left the mall as quickly as possible. He knew that since Trey was at the mall with Ab, now would be the perfect opportunity to act on something he'd had in play for the past couple of weeks. He knew they would take their time leaving in fear of him being near to strike. Joe's thinking was different. A bird in the hand was better than two in the bush. Opportunity couldn't have presented itself any better.

*****

Trina had been mentally wrestling with the same question for weeks—confronting Niki about Joe. She could see that it had been bothering them both. A few days prior, she and Joe went to lunch and he wasn't himself. The cold, calculated criminal everyone else saw when dealing with him disappeared when they were together. She saw a father that wanted to be a part of his daughter's life. She saw a ladies' man and a gentleman. She even saw a kind soul. It was amazing how one person could be so many different people depending on who he was dealing with.

He asked random questions regarding Niki as he picked over his food, questions she had answered on previous occasions; but she never tired at seeing him being so enthusiastic about anything or anyone. She grabbed hold of his hands so that he could sit still, "Joe, I can sit and talk with her."

Joe looked up and entangled eyes in a warm glare. "I don't want to mess up her head. It's not right." He looked away as his voice cracked, "We had a million chances to do right by her, and we made an excuse not to each and every time." He reached in his pocket and unfolded his money.

Trina knew where this conversation would lead next. He unraveled in excess of what was needed for lunch as he stood up and kissed her forehead. "You've been a friend to me. You never ask for more than you need, and you never lie to me." He turned and walked away as random men at nearby tables got up and scrambled to keep in pace with Joe to protect him.

*****

Quan felt himself slowly awakening but disoriented and confused. Everything appeared so dark and muffled. Voices were all that he could hear in the faint distance. Consciousness gradually revisited his limp frame. His eyes were fully open now, and he couldn't make out where he was. There were lights shining on him, and he was somehow shackled to his bed. Realizing that he was being restrained, Quan began jerking wildly. A short time after, he came to the realization of how futile it was. He was naked and the room was cold. He struggled to remember the last thing or place he was at.

Before a memory could register, he heard a man's voice approaching him. "Just in time for the party, young player." The voice didn't sound familiar or friendly. The position that Quan was being restrained in prohibited him from viewing whoever was speaking to him. He felt warm hands on his back, and ironically, chills raced through his body. He began to struggle for freedom. His struggle was met by a quick blow to the back of his head. The pain stiffened him instantly. Before he could recover, the hands began again. Slow moans escaped the man's lips as he appeared to enjoy the act more and more.

Quan was confused as to what was happening to him. The confusion was quickly eliminated when he felt fingers rubbing a cold gel like substance on his rectum. He fought back tears as the reality of what was occurring inserted itself in his mind. Within seconds, the man entered Quan with his hands firmly placed on his shoulders. The pain was unbearable. He slipped in and out of consciousness as the unknown assailant roughly delivered long, hard strokes to his anus.

For what felt like an eternity, Quan still held on, despite vomiting several times. His face was firmly pressed in it and made it difficult for him to breathe (the vomit). By now, there appeared to be spectators. Quan heard the voices clearly now, as if surround sound were installed in his head. "Look at our favorite playboy doing what he do best." Joe's voice was clear and evident. "Fucking," he continued. "This time, looks like you on the wrong end of the dick though." A hearty laugh followed joined by other laughter in unison. "Don't worry, young blood, I know how you like to tape these episodes so I took the liberty." Joe pointed to the lights, which Quan now recognized to be video cameras with spotlights. "I was unsure as to how you liked it, so I had to borrow yours to get it right." Joe revealed that he'd been behind the break-in and the tapes being missing. "Of course, I couldn't get it done without a little help." Joe pushed Dee closer to the bed so that Quan could see where his betrayal came from.

Dee's face shamefully drifted to the floor. Quan silently vowed to kill him personally if he got out this predicament. The smell of defecation and vomit blended for a putrid odor that became an intruder in the room. Joe, the twins, and two of his musclemen evacuated while leaving instruction for the sadistic rapist to finish up. The man went in and out of Quan's body while forcing him to look in his face, despite his eyes not being fully opened.

A dark slumber crept over Quan's awareness as he faded away from the scene. It all stopped as quickly as it started. The man draped a robe over his towering, muscular body, and disappeared into the night air. Joe left strict instructions with Dee to kill Quan. Dee had been promised two hundred and fifty thousand dollars for his act of betrayal. He just wanted to relocate and be done with this life.

He struggled to feel bad about it all, but reasoned at the thought when he remembered how Leslie's body still illuminated the corners of his mind. The support wasn't genuine, in his opinion. Trey treated her wake like a red carpet appearance. Quan hadn't sat his hormones aside to be a friend in his time of need. Ab, to him, it was just another opportunity to prove his loyalty. In all honesty, Dee was alone now that Leslie left this world.

He recycled his version of events in his head until it made sense to orchestrate this horror. He sat in a chair by the bed, eyeing Quan and preparing to give the final shot to his temple as he was advised. Joe had removed the cameras and left a car with the money in the trunk for his getaway. Dee snapped back to reality and cocked his gun back. He stood up and pointed. Seconds trailed by as he realized Quan didn't move a single muscle. He hadn't uttered a single sound. He was satisfied that Quan was dead already. He could start a new life beginning now.

Dee turned and raced out the door. Just as he was informed, a car was waiting for him with the keys in it. He got to the car and popped the trunk. Staring back at him was a black gym bag bulking from the sides. He was truly free. He closed the trunk and jumped in the car. Within minutes, Dee was on the highway headed to the airport. He cried profusely as he thought of his children, Leslie, and their life together torn apart, and no one seemed to be bothered at all he lost. Life had truly served him a mighty blow. Fate was cruel and unkind to each and every hustler alike, without discrimination.

Sirens cut his daydream short. He looked into his rearview to see two police cars. His heart dropped into his stomach where knots tightened and hardened. He hadn't cleaned off his gun and discarded it. There was no time at this point as the gun, sat snug on his waist-line. Dee hoped it would be a traffic stop that wouldn't interfere with his plan. After all, he had two hundred fifty thousand dollars in the trunk. He pulled over and waited for the officer to approach.

His life truly lay in the balance at this very moment. He wished he had driven slower. He wished previous years of training served him enough to clean and discard his gun. The pain of reality settled in quickly as two officers on opposing sides of the vehicle introduced themselves and requested his credentials. Dee, not being familiar with the car, fumbled through papers as he opened the glove compartment. There was only a single white envelope there that he removed to inspect. The officer on his side quickly commandeered it and opened. Within minutes, the cops had the trunk opened and unzipped Dee's black bag. It contained all guns—guns of different sizes, calibers, shapes, and even colors were jammed in the bag. Indeed, fate truly was cruel and unkind to each and every hustler alike.

The one gun Dee was worried about was nothing in comparison to the fifty-eight guns stuffed in the bag by Joe. No money, all guns. The guns were different guns used in killings on Trey and Quan's team over the past few months. Joe's plan called for the gun in Dee's waist to be the gun that killed Quan. That was something he calculated Dee to regret for the next fifty years of his life. The envelope in the glove compartment simply read, "Check the trunk."

Joe was smart enough to use Dee but not respect him for his disloyalty. Joe was wise enough to know that Dee was a weak link and had no place in a strong organization. His need for freedom of the life is what led him to his very imprisonment. He hoped Dee would see both the irony and the lesson. Never reveal your weakness to your enemy.

Dee cried like a newborn baby as the cops removed all the weapons from the vehicle. His betrayal delivered him to jail. Trey would have no trouble getting to him in there. Ab did enough time and had enough respect that it was just a matter of sending the word. In that moment, he feared for Trey. He was no match for Joe's intelligence and wisdom. Dee understood why Joe had sustained the last thirty-five years on the streets. It wasn't just sheer intelligence but tenacity and the ability to think the next three steps ahead. Joe knew Quan well enough to know that he couldn't resist the flesh and temptation of women. Twins would be far too much of an opportunity to pass up. Dee never knew the women. They were assassins that Joe flew in from Georgia. The art of seduction was more powerful than gunfire for a man of Quan's caliber.

*****

Trey had been calling Quan all day with no answer or return call. He sensed something was wrong. He wanted to share his news of the ring. Trey wanted to put together something extremely elaborate for Niki's return. She had given him a ring first and despite how good it made him feel, it was embarrassing to him as well. Having his lady in the world without a ring gave the wrong impression. Aside from that, Trey was slightly competitive in his love for her. He thought of sending horse and carriage to the airport to pick Niki up. Excitement overwhelmed him at the very thought of her return.

Quan jumped up in excruciating pain. Passing out truly saved his life. He surveyed the room for intruders or any sign of being alone. The house was empty. The crowd had left and took the cameras and crew with them. The only one left behind was the star of the show. Quan turned on his shower and sat in it. Everything replayed in his mind and his body was reminiscent of the events. His line of work was not conducive to what would be perceived as homosexual activity. He would lose the love and respect it took him a lifetime to build. In addition, no woman would ever take him seriously again.

The psychological effects immediately set in and destroyed his sanity. Quan washed for the next hour. He couldn't seem to rid himself of the smell. He contemplated his next step, and killing Dee personally was all that he could come up with. Quan went through his closet slowly as his limbs would not allow full movement and rotation. Being in the room alone conjured so many painful memories that all Quan could do was cry. He pulled together an outfit and dressed in the living room. There were a few things he valued sentimentally in the home that he would take. Aside from that he would have it cleaned by private maids and never return.

He searched for his phone, only to find he had thirty-seven missed calls. He was only concerned with calling Trey back. He hesitated. He called a hotel first to secure a room over the next month. He could barely hold a conversation without sniffling and crying. He couldn't conceive how he would make it in his line of work in this condition. He sat in a daze as his phone rang continuously from different callers. He couldn't bear to see a woman's name across the screen. Crying seemed to be his only defense to the attack on his self-esteem and life. He quickly decided to call Trey back before he called again.

"Bro, what up?" Quan forced himself to sound upbeat as Trey answered his call.

"Where in the fuck you been, dog?" Trey spat back, sounding very happy to hear from him.

"I was in here knocked out, it was a long night."

Trey assumed it was due to a woman or women even.

"Give me a chance to get myself right and we'll link later."

Trey agreed and the conversation ended.

This was harder than he thought. This was the biggest demon he'd have to fight yet. If the pain would physically subside, long enough for him to get dressed and get out the door, he would be grateful. Looking at his beautiful home, knowing it was defiled by such an intrusion, motivated him enough to start dressing. Questions raced through his mind. *How long was Dee playing both sides? Who else was a potential foe in disguise? Were Trey or Niki next?* Anger began taking the mood by surprise. He cringed at the thought of anything remotely similar happening to either of them.

Within minutes, Quan was dressed and lay slumped in his car, driving slowly. Tupac music was the soundtrack for the moment. He needed to hold on to his anger to fuel him through each moment. His gun rested on his lap, loaded.

*****

Ab was overseeing all the deals to re-up on product. They couldn't take the chance on being without it. Money and war went hand in hand, and without money to finance the war, they would be lost on more than one account. Only regular customers were being serviced. There was so much apprehension around anyone now that it just wasn't worth the risk. Casualties were popping up everywhere, and business was still doing well, at least for Trey and Quan.

Joe was so engulfed in the war that his profits suffered tremendously. His thinking was if he eliminated them, he would be able to get back what he lost and then some, due to the lack of competition. The strategy would prove brilliant if the plan only worked.

As Ab watched the last of the packages be loaded in four separate cars, his twenty-three gunmen spread out over the city were in place. Every step of the way, the cars communicated to each other, within the network of killers. Ab ensured a convoy of killers escorting death in the form of powder into the city's veins. As the last car left the scene, Ab crawled into his car and smiled with satisfaction. He wished that he was able to kill Joe in that mall, but he prayed opportunity would present itself again. He wasn't prepared to allow it to escape again.

*****

Trina had made her mind up to disobey Joe. She felt it for the greater good. Niki didn't respond to the call, so the voicemail picked up. "Baby, it's mama, no need to call back. Just stop by when you get a chance." Trina exhaled as she left the message. She felt one step closer to lifting a burden off her shoulders. This would incite hope in a way that only love could appreciate. Although this plan had the potential to backfire, she prayed the missing pieces of their lives would fill in the blanks. She convinced herself this would be a noble act rather than a disservice.

Trina felt confident and anxious in seeing her daughter. She would tell Niki and allow Niki to seek Joe out. Sitting both of them down was something Joe would never go for and, in fact, ran the risk of angering him. It was decided. Niki shall know who her father was!

*****

Quan sat at the light longer than he should have, staring into the crowd of older well-dressed men. Cars began blowing and honking their horns for the urgency of him moving. Quan opened his car door and began crossing the street with his weapon in hand. He raised and fired into the crowd. Those who were physically able scrambled for their lives, while the remaining men fell to death. It was truly a scene from a movie as cars slammed in reverse, screeching away from the scene. Before Quan could reach the curb for the last few men ducking behind cars, Ab pulled up in the middle of the street.

"Quan," he yelled out with two guns drawn moving in a circular motion. Quan turned and saw Ab coming toward him. He immediately dropped his weapon to his side and started walking toward Ab. When they reached each other, Ab grabbed Quan with one hand while moving back, waving his gun. He fired no shots as he noticed no threats amongst the men. He escorted Quan into his car and hurled his gun on the seat. Ab quickly went to the trunk and removed two grenades and pulled the pins. He ran over to Quan's car and threw them in. He then raced back to his car and pulled off quickly. "Gimme your gun, dude," Ab ordered with his hand out as Quan's car exploded into pieces in the rearview mirror. He noticed

Quan was disheveled and didn't necessarily resemble his daily style and charisma. His trained eye took notice to Quan's wrists where he could tell something bruised him from a restraint. "Any reason you shooting an Elk's club up?"

Quan offered a delayed response as he stared in a daze. "Joe's men," he softly uttered. Ab didn't correct him. They drove for a few miles and Ab asked the question that been burning his mind. "Where's Dee?"

Quan looked at him as serious as possible and simply stated, "Living a dead man's life."

Ab smiled devilishly. "Say no more."

*****

Trey leaned his head back and gripped the basketball with firmness, raised his arms, and thrust the ball through the hoop. He smiled as he quickly ran to retrieve the ball. A small team of armed men clapped, cheering him on.

Ab raced in the gym with his gun drawn. Everyone abruptly stopped and reached for their weapons. "Nah, niggas, y'all too late." The gym fell silent as Ab continued speaking, "Y'all in here tryna be cheerleaders and shit, occupying both hands which leave my nigga exposed. Shameful shit if you ask me."

Every man in attendance respected Ab's expertise enough to accept the constructive criticism. Ab approached Trey as he dribbled the ball and made attempts to take it from him. Trey's smooth style of trickery dribble and ball control proved too much for Ab. They laughed like teenagers on a school's yard.

Quan burst in and ran straight for the ball. "Oh, this ya back up, bro?" Trey laughed at Ab. The next hour unfolded as the childhood friends enjoyed a competitive game of basketball. As usual, Trey won, but Quan had the most fun. As the entire team prepared to leave, Trey turned to Quan and asked, "Where's Dee?"

Ab answered on his behalf, "We'll talk later."

Trey knew what that meant, and it didn't feel good knowing Dee was at the other end of that conversation. He noticed that his work ethic had been slacking at best lately but afforded him patience since Leslie was killed.

Trey put both his hands on Quan's shoulders. "Where the hell you been, bro? I needed you for something big."

Quan smiled and nodded, "What up? I got a lil niece or nephew on the way?"

"Let's not jump the gun," chuckled Trey. "I did get the ring though."

Quan stopped short and found no words to express his happiness for Trey and Niki. He came closer and hugged Trey. The hug was cut short by an awkwardness of Trey simply touching Quan's back. He tried to snatch away unnoticeably. In the moment, he struggled with whether he should talk to Trey about what happened. It's not that he didn't trust him with the information; he just didn't have the nerve to speak on it just yet.

Quan momentarily relapsed to the moment where he was alone and vulnerable. He crystalized the moment that no one came to save him. He blamed himself, mentally replaying all the moments that led up to it, and there were signs to reveal the road ahead. Quan's focus was just misplaced. He looked at Trey and spoke seriously, "My nigga, promise me something."

Trey stared back with the same seriousness. "Anything, you name it."

"If ever I need you, be there."

Trey didn't question where this came from. He only leaned in and spoke, "I'll come running if I'm not already by your side."

Quan was satisfied. They emptied the gym and filed in cars to form their convoy.

*****

Different flight numbers were being called out as people hustled back and forth to make their destinations. Niki sat in the airport and watched each man pass her by as she awaited her flight. She took notice of their facial features and likened them to hers. She wondered if any one of these men could be her father. She imagined what it would have been like to have him there all along—bike rides in the park, ice-cream cones with sprinkles, recitals and rehearsals while his proud face stared back from the audience. She imagined her father walking her down the aisle at her wedding. She imagined him whispering to her, "Baby girl, I'm so proud of you," while he fought back tears. Her imagination painted vivid pictures of a loving father who was overprotective, stern, loving, supportive and...well, like Trey. Her thoughts smoothly transitioned to Trey and his scent, his touch. He spoke to her as if it were poetry being recited. He touched her like pure white silk.

Her flight couldn't come fast enough. She wanted to return home to her reality. She wanted to fly back early and surprise him but was too excited to let him know that she was en route.

*****

Dee sat in a cell not far from home. All he could do was cry. All the decisions and actions that provided a segue for this moment made guest appearances in his head. His role was comprised of a stellar performance. It entailed betrayal, deception, sex, money, murder, and punishment. The latter was his reality. Fear paralyzed him as he sat on the cold metal bench. Different prisoners passed while peering into his holding cell. Some faces he knew, and some faces knew him. He spoke to none as they yelled for his attention or greeted him. He assumed the word was already out and any one of the men were sent to execute his demise.

Dee shivered and shook as his cries began to carry from cell to cell. The guard appeared and immediately began taunting Dee. "You want me to send you in some company to talk about it? Maybe wipe those tears?" The guy laughed and walked away, looking over his shoulder at the pitiful sight. He had seen it a hundred times before. The toughest of criminals weakened instantly by these walls. The sounds that escaped and haunted the halls and sectors were all too familiar to him. Dee didn't see this bend in the road. Somewhere in his travels, he had definitely taken a wrong turn.

*****

The shower stole the tension from Trey's back and arms. The workout from basketball was just what he needed to ease his mind. He planned to take Niki to dinner when she returned. Leaving the restaurant, horse pulled carriages would await their riders. The horse ride would lead them to Central Park to an opening where a band played her favorite song—"Gotta be" by Jagged Edge. A trail of roses would lead her from the carriage to the bench near the band. That's where her life would forever change.

Trey meticulously planned. He had implemented several of his own ideas infused by movie scenes and what he knew about his woman. There would be a photographer to capture the entire event in which they would have the pictures turned into invitations and mailed to would-be guests of the wedding. Trey knew that he would have to include Trina. She and Niki were too close to exclude her. The plan was immaculate. The competiveness in him told him that his version of the proposal would make for a better story when told to their children twenty years from now.

*****

"Flight 613 to Newark's EWR to begin boarding in fifteen minutes."

Niki was queued to call her mother back before boarding. She had been too caught up to call back, although she heard the message. There were no telltale signs of what she could have wanted by the message she left. "Hello, Momma!" she yelled into the phone as Trina answered.

"Hey, baby, I been looking forward to sitting with you."

Niki smiled and answered promptly, "I got your message, and just as soon as I kiss my husband, I'll be there."

Trina loved to hear that Niki was so happy. She felt her job as a parent was done well. She just needed to complete her requirement as a mother. While Niki had been gone, she could only think of her. No matter how good of a mother she had been, she could never replace her father. "Well, I'll be here. We'll make a day of it."

Niki was excited and agreed as she rushed to her flight home.

A long exhale and a sigh of relief overcame Trina as she reflected on her conversation with Niki. This was really happening. After all these years, all the days and nights that she toiled over this decision, the turmoil that it had incited in her was unreal. She had no one to tell the good news to. This secret had been weighing on her heavily over the years. As of late, she realized that everyone had the right to know where they came from. Good, bad, or indifferent, everyone deserved to know. Her baby girl would soon get her chance.

*****

Horns and screeches followed Trey throughout the city as he whisked in and out of traffic to complete his errands for Niki. Ab was used to his driving and was unaffected as he watched the cars in traffic and people moving around them. He couldn't help but smile while looking at Trey. He was obviously happy.

Ab loved and admired his dear friend. He always thought this level of happiness required a sacrifice of one or more of your sense that you needed for survival. He couldn't afford to be that happy. He preferred to survive. It wouldn't be fair to use the terminology *live* because how could one truly live without knowing true love? He admired Trey for being able to balance the two. He loved him for different reasons. He, Trey, and Quan had been friends since they were all children. Not one disagreement ever split their bond. Those were spectacular odds.

Since his initial plans, Trey had incorporated caterers for a celebration dinner. He would have exotic birds flown in as well as rare flowers, limos, and gifts for everyone that made this a reality. No expense was spared to secure that smile on Niki's face. Fueled with an undying love infused by missing her and combined with understanding what she meant to his life, Trey carried out each task as if it was the actual wedding he was planning. Making sure his proposal was better than hers would be an added bonus.

Since running into Joe at the mall, and Dee no longer being considered part of the family, Ab decided to become more visual in protecting Trey. He hoped his expertise and presence alone would fend off certain unskilled killers. The skilled opponents he welcomed. He hadn't decided what to do with Dee as of yet, but he knew that his body would be left in front of the house he grew up in. It was their unique way of sending a message to people from their crew. It was a surefire way to deter any against betrayal.

They had to make time to sit down with Quan and get more details, but it would have to just be the three of them. Whatever ousted Dee, it was classified information on a need-to-know basis.

With only the caterer and a payment and contract signing for the wild animals, Trey's work was almost done. His phone rang and Niki's face boasted her beauty on his profile picture. "Hey, my lady," he answered in a hurried tone.

"Guess who's back!" She harmonized to the tune of a familiar rap song.

Trey smiled and asked, "Where are you?"

Niki grabbed the last of her luggage from the conveyor belt as she replied, "On my way home, I'll see you there shortly."

Trey became slightly frustrated at her assuming he was free enough to stop what he was doing and just come home. His frustration quickly subsided at the realization that she was actually back within his reach. This was the first time he had been apart from her. His car turned in the direction of their home as he slowed his pace. "My nigga, why you think we do all we do?" he asked Ab from nowhere. Before a response was offered, he continued "I mean, we first started out for sneakers and gear money, but then this got bigger than all four of us and we had more than we could ever anticipate."

Ab listened, unsure if he was supposed to answer or if it was rhetorical. "What don't you have right now today that you can't buy or send someone to go get for you, my nigga?"

Ab turned to Trey while lowering the volume on the radio. "Brethren, you spend half your life trying to accumulate items, people, things, then you spend the rest of your life trying to protect it all. As long as you living, you have to protect who you are, what you have, and what you love."

Trey smiled as Ab's words set in. It made sense coming from him and sounded so insightful. He pulled up to the house as he noticed Niki removing her luggage from the trunk of her car. "Pretty lady like you should have someone to do these type of things in life for you," Trey shouted from across the street.

Niki turned and smiled. "I actually do," she stated calmly as she dropped her bags and waited for Trey to come over. Trey and Niki's lips met as if it were the first time and exploded on contact. They lost the world as they kissed and hugged. The noise was drowned out, and the reality of the city street became a fairytale land as a king and queen exchanged words, ideas made through lip contact.

Ab walked up and grabbed Niki's bags as he spoke, "Welcome home, punk." He smirked as he moved around them and went upstairs. He thought it would be better to be first to enter the house anyway.

Moments later, the couple stared into each other's eyes as they fixed on each other in a daze. Marriage was so important to the both of them, and the only thing standing in their way was time. The seconds that impregnated minutes which gave birth to hours between now and forever kept the couple from becoming official. Niki's phone was the first to ring, immediately followed by Trey's.

Trina was reminding Niki of their commitment, while the caterer was Trey's interruption. The two made a promise to meet back at home as soon as possible and consummate their love. Trey watched Niki get back into her car and take off as quickly as she had come. He called Ab down so that they could make their way to the caterer.

Minutes later, Ab and Trey sat at a light in traffic, awaiting the green signal. The tide shifted in their favor as Joe himself came out the store on the adjacent corner. He appeared to have only one gunman with him. Trey and Ab noticed him simultaneously and smiled at one another. Ab was the driver and he quickly pulled through the light and placed Joe in the rear view. They had only seconds to act. If he got in the car, it would result in a street chase, and this time of day would be a bad idea for that. Trey cocked back his weapon and began opening the door.

Ab grabbed his arm. "Nah, think about it. Would I leave you alone?" The response resonated in Trey's mind as Ab furthered his argument. "No way he doesn't have eyes or muscle on him. You'd be walking into a trap." Trey saw the logic and did the unthinkable. He tossed his gun on the seat and got out the car.

Joe was crossing the street toward the two when he realized Trey was coming at him. He swung his head around to weigh his odds. He noticed Trey's hands up in a surrendering motion. He stopped in his tracks and watched for a second. Joe was without a weapon himself in fear of police random searches. Ab ran up behind Trey with his gun drawn, and three guys appeared from the crowd, aiming back at them. "No, Ab, fall back," Trey shouted. He continued toward Joe with his hands clearly raised so Joe would feel comfortable.

Joe made no effort to call off his men at first. Trey reached him and they stood face-to-face. "How long does this need to go on?" Trey asked while showing no signs of fear.

Joe waved his men off and the weapons were lowered. Joe stood silent for the next few moments. He was slightly embarrassed that he was not able to eliminate his opponent with so much effort and planning. He assumed Trey had got the news about Quan's death and decided to concede. "This can end now if you can respect a few things."

Trey wasn't accustomed to being spoken to in that tone, but he managed to keep cool and ask, "Like?"

Joe answered quickly, "Let's see if we can put together a real estate plan that will give us both operating room."

Trey thought to himself and extended his hand to Joe. Ab's head dropped as he watched from a distance, not being able to hear the words exchanged. Joe went into his suit pocket while yelling out to Ab, "I'm gon get myself a pen out my suit pocket, young blood." Joe removed the pen and jotted down an address. He shoved the paper in Trey's hand and advised him, "Come by tonight 'bout 7:30 so we can make some progress."

Trey nodded in approval, turned, and walked away. Trey was relieved. Although this wasn't something he set out to do, the same way he spotted Joe, it was possible for Joe to spot him; or even worse, Niki. The city was becoming too small for all the men to be giants. He would discuss the decision with Quan before finalizing.

Joe assumed Quan's death was a message that prompted the surrender and would deliver a truce. His strategy was brilliant, or so he thought.

*****

Quan began drinking in his hotel room soon after seeing Trey and Ab. He drank in excess to drown the thoughts and the pain. His mind enhanced the act and replayed in slow motion over and over again. He thought to himself what he would do differently if he could just have another chance. He toiled over the entire situation. Quan drank until he convinced himself to go back to the house in which it all happened. He grabbed two guns and a half-empty bottle of Hennessy and began driving to his old home. Thoughts of revenge and death planted seeds in his mind until he couldn't think of anything but.

A simple hug from Trey triggered feelings that rendered him incapable of handling. Playing basketball was far too much of a contact activity between two men. For days, he had been ignoring calls from girls. He watched pornos to see if he was able to get an erection. There lay more discomfort for him. He couldn't manufacture the words to describe the event that occurred to him. The pain was too much for one man.

Once he reached the house, as the key unlocked the door, he could almost smell the odor again. He became nauseous as he attempted to retrace his steps. He cursed himself for ever pursuing the twins. He practically gave himself up. Tears streamed as the memory repeated itself. Quan convinced himself that he would be able to live without the thought of it all if only his mind had no trace of the event. He went to his guest bathroom and lifted the false ceiling. He then removed a kilo of cocaine and took it to his office area and threw it on the desk.

Quan removed a knife and slit the bag. The cocaine crumbs remaining on the knife were lifted and placed to the edge of his nose. He took one long snort and it disappeared in his nose. The room boasted with accomplishment as the author of this tale penned a sad song of woe and disgrace. His thoughts crystalized as he searched for his liquor bottle. He placed his gun on the desk next to the cocaine and repeated more drinking and snorting. Pain and sobs filled the air to mix with sodomy, deceit, power, and defeat. The cocaine sharpened Quan's senses like a knife on a jagged rock. Then the thoughts returned with vengeance.

*****

Niki removed her pocketbook from the passenger seat of her car and opened the door. Her mother was standing on the curb awaiting her. Niki could tell Trina had been crying. She approached quickly. "What's wrong, Ma?" She hugged her and wiped her face.

"Baby, for once, everything is right." Trina smiled back and grabbed Niki's arm while leading her in the house. They reached the comfort of Trina's home and sat. She didn't want to hesitate, so she started right away, "Baby, you have a father."

Niki's eyes became teary as she listened, as if her life depended on it. "Your father loves you very much, and he wants to be a part of your life." Trina, barely able to continue speaking, handed Niki an envelope and broke down.

"Mama why would you keep this from me?" Niki stood and screamed frantically. "You had no right! You don't know what my life has been like without knowing!" Niki collapsed on her mother and cried profusely.

Trina knew the moment would be too emotional to explain everything in detail. She decided to write down an address to find Joe so he could explain personally.

Niki was angry at her mother. So much of her life was missing without knowing who her father was. She looked at today's sequence of events as God answering her prayers after so many sleepless nights and examining strange men's faces.

"I'm sorry baby, I'm so sorry," Trina cried as she hit the floor in a fetal position. Niki stood up and stuffed the envelope in her pocketbook and ran out.

*****

Trey counted out the cash for the caterer and shoved the money across the counter. The caterer, not bothering to count it, began writing a receipt and confirmed the menu for a final time. He went to the top drawer and pulled out a CD and handed it to Trey along with the receipt. Trey looked puzzled at the disc.

"This is a bonus, young brother" the caterer exclaimed as he smiled. Trey stood and shook his hand and nodded toward Ab.

Before Trey ran into Joe, Joe had paid the caterer to give Trey the disc. It contained the entire ordeal of Quan's rape. Joe hoped it would send Trey into a rage and lose composure of how the war should be handled. This, he hoped, would make it easier to kill him.

As he and Ab reached the car, they joked of how surprised Niki would be at what was in store. They envisioned dancing and singing and an evening of fun. As their bodies were met by the smooth, soft leather, Trey slid the disc in the player while Ab placed his weapon between the two of them for easy access. "Bro, we might not even need to do this no more," Trey said as he pointed to the gun.

Ab turned and looked at him unaffected, "I'll never get that comfortable." The mood shifted instantly as Trey noticed Quan lying naked on the bed held down in restraints. His heart dropped at what took place next as he watched, crying and saying no as if Quan could hear him or stop it.

Ab looked on in disbelief. He shed no tear but he was angered from within. Trey assumed his meet later with Joe was obviously a trap. They watched in horror as every detail unfolded before their eyes. Both their hearts sank deep in the seats when Dee could be seen visibly on screen. It made sense why he wasn't with Quan now.

Trey looked at Ab for a reaction. "I didn't know. He never mentioned."

Trey called Quan, while fumbling in his pocket for the paper that Joe gave him. "This bastard's been playing us all along, dog!" Trey yelled while waiting for Quan to pick up.

Ab instinctively started making his way to Quan's house. Trey ordered Ab to pull over so that he could gather his thoughts. Quan didn't answer. They both got out and stood on the curb in apparent shock from what they witnessed. Quan's call shook the moment as Trey answered in a hurry. "Quan," was all Trey could find the strength to say.

"Bro, you remember I told you if ever I needed you…"

Trey yelled back, "Where you at, man?"

Quan continued, "If ever there was a time I needed you, it's now." He terminated the call. Suicide was the only thought that now introduced itself to Quan's logic. The drugs and alcohol along with what had occurred had pushed him to a place he couldn't return from.

Trey jumped in the car and grabbed the wheel and began a wild drive to Quan's house. He grabbed the gun and raced through the streets, disobeying every traffic signal. The police took pursuit within minutes. Ab held on and watched while he hoped for the best.

*****

Quan had finally reached breaking point when he realized there were footsteps stampeding up the stairway toward his door. He hastened his decision, for he knew that it was Trey, and although he loved Trey like a brother, he couldn't turn back. He gently placed the gun to his head. Without closing his eyes or even bracing himself for the unimaginable, Quan eased the trigger until the gun sent shockwaves out into the hallway, to Trey and Ab who rushed up the stairs. As they burst through the door, weapons drawn, the sight weakened Trey instantly. His boy lay lifeless on the expensive rug as his life escaped into the atmosphere. Before Trey could reach the pool of blood and matter that was once Quan, the police came storming in and it all became a blur.

*****

Ab took the blame for the chase and the gun. The police happily arrested him. They asked Trey question after question and forced him off what they called a crime scene. Pain guided him to his car where he sat a few seconds and stared at his phone. He had missed eighteen calls from Niki. This was the first time ever he couldn't stomach talking to her.

He pulled the paper from his pocket and drove at a reasonable pace to the address Joe provided. Once he arrived, he went into the trunk and placed two weapons on his sides. He closed the trunk and exhaled. He stared at the building and started in.

Joe was there alone. Since he and Trey agreed to talk, he had given his guys the night off. He sat and listened to Trina explained to him that Niki would be arriving shortly. His body was numb from the news. Joe was truly vulnerable.

*****

Niki was truly afraid to go meet this man without Trey. She had called for his company several times, and he didn't answer. She went in the trunk and removed her small caliber pistol that he provided her with for protection. She drove to the address Trina gave her, crying and overwhelmed with emotion. Niki would finally meet her father. The only other man she needed by her side was her husband-to-be.

*****

Trey walked in as Joe held the phone to his ear. He had left all the doors open, expecting Niki, not Trey. His eyes widened as Trey neared him, gun drawn. It dawned on Joe that Trey had never intended on a truce but only wanted him to let his guard down. Trey truly had the drop on Joe. Trey cried as he neared him, thinking of what he had put Quan through. No words were spoken by either party as Trey closed in on his prey.

*****

Niki pulled up and tucked her gun in slowly. She got out and wiped her tears and made her way up the stairs. She walked slowly as the tears began again. Two shots rang out and Niki reached for her gun. She heard a man's voice that sounded like Trey, and she quickened her pace. When she got to the top of the stairs, she saw Trey walking toward her with his gun lying on the floor behind him.

In the chair slumped over was Joe. Niki recognized him and began yelling, "Daddy!"

Trey looked up, surprised to see Niki, and began moving toward her. She raised her gun and fired until the gun went empty. The room was filled with life escaping into the atmosphere.

In his final moments of his life, Joe watched his only daughter come to him and defend his life.

In Trey's final moments, he watched the only woman he ever lived for kill him. Before he could realize what was happening, death came swiftly and removed him.

*****

The officer removed the cuffs from Ab's wrists as he finalized the arrest process. He placed him in a holding cell with one other prisoner. Ab sat and watched the officer disappear down the long hallway. The other prisoner's crying caused Ab to walk over and tower over him.

Dee lifted his head in shock. Ab removed his belt, wrapped it around his hands, and began strangling Dee until no life was within his chest.

ABOUT THE AUTHOR

Infused with music, influenced by poetry and controlled by writing, your author is a trifecta of words and rhythm swirled into a melodic tune of artistry! Each work is designed to be a tapestry of words, arranged to align your emotions with your attention. A Newark native, who is also a DJ and producer, is sharing his greatest joy with an array of readers and determined to satisfy each one. Until the next adventure. Thanks for tuning in!